Jennifer Bohnet is originally from the West Country but now lives in the wilds of rural Brittany, France. She's still not sure how she ended up there! The saying 'life is what happens while you're deciding what to do…' is certainly true in her case. She's always written alongside having various jobs: playgroup leader, bookseller, landlady, restauranteur, farmer's wife, secretary – the list is endless but does provide a rich vein of inspiration for her stories.

Allergic to housework and gardening she rarely does either, but she does like cooking and entertaining and wandering around *vide greniers* (the French equivalent of flea markets) looking for a bargain or two. Her children currently live in fear of her turning into an ageing hippy and moving to Totnes, Devon.

To find out more about Jennifer visit her website at jenniferbohnet.com or chat to her on Twitter at @jenniewriter.

THE
Little Kiosk
BY THE SEA

Jennifer Bohnet

ONE PLACE. MANY STORIES

HarperCollins PUBLISHERS
Since 1817

This novel is entirely a work of fiction. The names, characters
and incidents portrayed in it are the work of the author's
imagination. Any resemblance to actual persons, living or
dead, events or localities is entirely coincidental.

HQ
An imprint of HarperCollins*Publishers* Ltd.
1 London Bridge Street
London SE1 9GF

This paperback edition 2017

1

First published in Great Britain by
HQ, an imprint of HarperCollins*Publishers* Ltd. 2015

Copyright © Jennifer Bohnet 2015

Jennifer Bohnet asserts the moral right to be
identified as the author of this work.
A catalogue record for this book is
available from the British Library.

ISBN: 978-1-84845-715-7

Printed and bound by
CPI Group (UK) Ltd, Croydon, CR0 4YY

This one is for my daughter Emily and my son Nicholas
– my very own Dartmothians!

EARLY SEASON

PROLOGUE

For as long as anyone could remember, the kiosk on the quay had been part of the town's summer street furniture. A focal point for the locals as much as the holidaymakers. Every 1st March, the wooden hexagonal hut reappeared without fuss or fanfare on its designated place on the embankment between the taxi rank and the yacht club, its wooden struts and panels gleaming with freshly applied paint. Red, white, blue and yellow – all bright summer colours which, come October, would have been bleached and faded away by the summer weather. The jet-black orb on the top of the domed roof was a favourite with the gulls, who perched there serenely surveying the scene before swooping down and stealing ice creams and pasties from unwary holidaymakers.

As well as its annual paint make-over, the kiosk had occasionally been refurbished inside. These days it boasted an electric connection for the necessary computer, a kettle, mugs, a round tin that was never empty of biscuits and a small electric heater to keep the occupant warm in early and late season when the wind off the river blew straight in through the half-open stable door.

There was a small shelf unit for holding tickets and the cash box, a cupboard for locking things in, space to the left of the door for the outside advertising boards to come in overnight and three foldaway canvas director chairs for sitting outside in the sun with friends when business was slow.

The whole atmosphere of the town changed as the locals welcomed the reappearance of the hut which signalled the imminent arrival of the holidaymakers, the second home owners and the day-trippers. Maybe this would be the year fortunes would be made. If not fortunes, at least enough money to see the families through winter without getting deep into overdrafts. The last thing anyone wanted – or needed – was another wet season.

This summer though, 1st March came and went with no sign of the kiosk. All winter, rumours had rumbled around town about its demise and locals feared the worst: the council had never liked it and wanted it gone – not true, the mayor said; Health and Safety had condemned it as an unfit workplace – but nobody would give details of the problem; the rent for the summer season had doubled and Owen Hutchinson, owner of the pleasure boats he operated through the kiosk, had refused to pay. A fact he denied.

Then, two weeks before Easter, without any warning, the re-painted kiosk appeared in its usual place. Collectively, the town heaved a sigh of relief. Panic over. Time to enjoy the summer.

Chapter One

Sabine

'Two tickets for the afternoon river trip? No problem,' Sabine said, smiling at the young woman standing in front of the kiosk. 'Here you go. We cast off at 2.30 today, so make sure you're back here at least fifteen minutes before.'

'Definitely. We'll be here. It won't be rough, will it?' the girl asked as she handed over the ticket money. 'I'm not a very good sailor. We're down on holiday and my boyf... my husband loves boats so I thought I'd treat him.' She looked along the embankment. 'He's wandered off to look at some old steam engine or something.'

'The river will be as smooth as the proverbial baby's bottom this afternoon,' Sabine promised.

'Great. I'd hate to spoil things by being sea sick.'

'On honeymoon, are we?' Sabine said, looking at the shiny ring on the girl's left hand.

The girl flushed. 'How'd you guess?'

'Oh something to do with the way you forgot to call him your husband? You obviously haven't had time to get used to saying it yet.'

'Two days,' the girl confided. She leant in. 'We eloped.'

'Very brave of you,' Sabine said, smiling.

The girl shrugged. 'Necessity rather than bravery,' she said. 'See you this afternoon.'

Sabine watched her walk away and join her new husband, who greeted her with a lingering kiss. 'May married life be kind to you,' she muttered before turning her attention back to sorting the kiosk out for the season.

Two weeks late arriving on the quay meant there'd barely been time to set up things before the first river trip of the season. Not that there was a lot to do really, but Sabine liked to have everything to hand. Ticket books, cash tin, receipt book, tide table book, chalk, mugs, foldaway chairs, kettle, bottles of water, coffee and biscuits. That just left finding space for the first four paintings of the season.

A couple of years ago, she'd discovered the tourists liked her pencil sketches of the town and the river. One quiet afternoon she'd sat in one of the canvas director's chairs outside the kiosk and idly started to sketch the river and its boats. She'd wanted a small picture to hang in her newly decorated bathroom, with its blue and white nautical theme. A tourist collecting tickets for a boat trip had seen it and asked to buy it when finished – provided she'd sign it for him.

That initial sale had thrown her into a panic. She'd no idea what to charge for an unframed original picture. It wasn't as if she was famous or anything – or likely to be. In the end she suggested a sum and the tourist had shaken his head at her – before giving her double what she had asked and saying, 'You really don't know how talented you are, do you?'

Sabine had taken the money thoughtfully. Yes, she did know she had a talent. Years ago she'd been all set to go to art college but instead had to give up her place and stay at home to help look after her mother. Something that she'd done willingly.

By the time she was free to pursue a career, the time to go to art college had passed and marriage and family life had eventually taken over. If she drew anything in the following years it was simply because she fancied doing it.

After that first, unexpected sale, she'd started to do a couple of drawings a week, surprised by how quickly they sold. These days she spent winter painting and drawing views of the town and the river, ready for summer. By the end of the season she rarely had any left. Her secret 'just for fun' bank account grew substantially every summer.

The one she hung now on the folded-back stable door was a firm favourite with the tourists. A pen and ink drawing of the old Butterwalk with its columns and hanging baskets, it sold well every season.

Once she was satisfied the picture was hanging straight, she stood with her back to the kiosk looking across the river and along the embankment, breathing deeply and thinking about the future. Was this really going to be the last season she'd be working in the kiosk? If the council carried out their threat at the end of summer, forcing Owen and the other boat owners to use an un-imaginative refurbished office on the other side of the road, it would be. No way could she bear the thought of working indoors all summer long. Still Owen and the Robertsons were on the case, demanding a public meeting before a decision was taken and getting up a petition.

A flash of red coming towards her caught her eye. She laughed and shook her head. Johnnie, her twin brother. The old Breton red beret sitting jauntily on his head and the folder of papers he was carrying told her instantly this morning he was on the 'Save the Kiosk' warpath. Five minutes later he was greeting her with his customary cheek kisses. They might have been born in the town, but their French father had ensured they knew all about their French ancestry and learnt the language. For years now, they'd spoken only French to each other in private.

'*Ça va?*'

'*Oui. Et toi?*'

Johnnie LeRoy nodded.

'Haven't seen that for a few years,' she said, looking at the beret. 'Thought we'd thrown it out when Papa died.'

'Never,' Johnnie said, shaking his head. 'Family heirloom. Sign of the workers' solidarity this is.'

Sabine smiled. She doubted that any of the locals would realise the significance of the red beret.

'Got a few signatures already,' Johnnie said opening the folder and handing her a poster with the words, 'SAVE THE KIOSK' emblazoned in red across the top. 'Need you to pin this up and to put the petition somewhere people can sign it.'

'You don't think the powers-that-be are serious about getting rid of the kiosk?'

Johnnie shrugged. 'Don't know. Telling them we want it kept won't do any harm though. Embankment wouldn't be the same without the kiosk.'

'True. Fancy a coffee?' Sabine asked, reaching for the kettle.

Johnnie shook his head. 'Not this morning, thanks. I want to drop a poster off at the yacht club and then I'm planning on giving Annie and her bottom a good going-over.'

Sabine smiled at the scandalised expression on a passing tourist's face. Johnnie grinned at her before whispering, 'Gets them every time!' Annie, named after his late wife, was Johnnie's thirty-two-foot sailing yacht moored out on one of the pontoons in the river.

'Have fun. See you tonight for supper,' she said. Turning her attention to a couple looking at the times of river trips for the week, she began to talk them into taking the afternoon trip. Gift of the gab, Owen called her sales technique. Said it was the main reason he employed her to run the kiosk. That and the fact he was in love with her. She'd lost count of the number of times he'd asked her to marry him since Dave died. Said he was going to keep asking her until she said yes.

It had become something of a joke between them now. Only last week he'd asked her again and she'd said her usual 'No', adding jokingly, 'I think you'd better stop asking me, Owen. Otherwise one of these days I might be tempted to say yes and then you'll be saddled with me.'

'If that means there is a possibility of you saying yes one day, I intend to keep on asking,' Owen had replied seriously. 'I've always loved you. Dave was my best mate but I could have killed him when you married him and not me.'

Sabine sighed. 'Owen, I love you to bits but not in that way. You deserve more than a one-sided marriage.'

'If you were the one side, I'd take it happily,' Owen said.

Sorrowfully Sabine shook her head at him before reaching up and giving him a kiss on the cheek. 'Sorry, Owen.' She knew she hurt him every time she refused his offer, but love had to be a two-way thing for a marriage to work, didn't it? She'd been a single woman for so long she could barely remember what it had been like being in a relationship, let alone being married.

When Dave had died, it had been a devastated Owen who'd tried to step into his shoes and be there whenever Peter had needed a father figure, insisting that was what godfathers were for. Two years ago he'd made sure Peter had a job ready and waiting for him when he'd finished his engineering course at college. At the time she'd questioned Owen as to whether it was a genuine job or one he created.

'Of course it's genuine,' he'd said. 'I need a boat engineer. Happy for it to be Peter. Besides,' he added with a grin, 'a bit of nepotism never did any harm!' It was Peter's second season this year and he'd told Sabine he loved it. Couldn't imagine doing anything else – living anywhere else.

She did wish sometimes that Peter had been a bit more adventurous – left home and seen a bit of the world before settling down in town. He'd done a couple of yacht deliveries with Johnnie but hadn't wanted to do more. Took after his father in that respect. Dave had never wanted to live anywhere else or even take holidays abroad, whereas she had always longed to see the world. The one opportunity to do that had sadly come at the wrong time of her life.

She glanced at a tourist studying the sailing timetable.

'Can I book a ticket for this afternoon's trip?' he asked, his accent marking him as American.

'Of course.'

'Great little town you've got here,' he said, as Sabine took his money and handed him a ticket.

'Your first visit?'

'Yeah, hoping to unearth some relatives,' he said with a grin. 'Grandmother was a GI bride way back in '44. She kind of lost touch with folks here when she left. Family name was Holdsworth. Don't suppose it's yours? Know anyone of that name?'

Sabine laughed. 'Well-connected ancestors you've got with that name, that's for sure. No, it's not mine. And as this isn't small-town America, I don't know everyone, but I don't think there are any Holdsworths currently living in town.'

'You mean there's no longer a Govenor Holdsworth in charge out at the castle? I was hoping for an invite to stay there.'

'You wouldn't be very comfortable if you did – Windsor Castle it's not.'

'Shame. Good job I booked into The Royal for a week or two then. See you later.'

By the time Sabine helped Owen and Peter to cast off that afternoon, the boat was three quarters full and she watched it depart, pleased the first of the season's sailings was so full.

As the Queen of the River began to make its way upstream, Sabine started to close up the kiosk. Life for the next few months would be ruled by the tide table and the need to open the kiosk every day to take advance bookings. Today, though, it was early enough in the season, with few people around, she could close up and go home for an hour or two before the boat returned and she had to be on hand to help the passengers disembark.

A chilly March breeze was blowing off the river and Sabine was glad of her fleece as she made for her cottage halfway up Crowthers Hill, one of the old roads leading out of town into the back country.

The house in Above Town she and Dave had bought together as a newly married couple had been too full of memories for both her and Peter to stay there happily without Dave. Far better to have a new start in a different house – one that she and Peter could build into a home. So twelve years ago she'd bought the cottage when Dave's insurance money had eventually turned up.

Johnnie and Annie helped with getting the place habitable – it had been empty for two years and took weeks of hard work from the three of them to make it habitable – and she and Peter had lived there ever since.

Johnnie alone was responsible for the attic conversion three years ago. Sabine had watched in despair as her lovely, kind, compassionate brother all but followed his wife into an early grave. Finding him, bottle in hand, wandering around town at two o'clock one afternoon barely able to stand, she threatened him with dire consequences if he didn't stop.

'Did you see me doing this when I lost Dave? No. It's hard but you've just got to get on with it.'

'You had Peter,' he'd muttered. 'Perhaps if we'd had a child I'd have something to live for.'

'You think it was easier because I had a child? Dream on. It was harder. A constant reminder of what I'd lost. He needed to grieve too. You've still got a lot of life to live so don't give me that bullshit about not having anything to live for. I'm still here loving you and so is Peter.'

Shouting and yelling at him to get a grip hadn't made any difference so, in the end, Sabine had taken action the only way she knew – she gave Johnnie something practical to do. Not daring to think about him drinking when he was away on a trip, she cancelled all his yachting work for six months. Then she bullied him into doing her attic conversion, insisting he moved in with her while he did it. That way she could monitor his alcohol, keep an eye on him and feed him regular meals.

Nine hard months it took, but at the end he'd hammered and sawn his way out of his grief and Sabine had a studio in the attic with a view of the river. More important, Johnnie was on his way back to living life. These days he lived mostly on board his boat despite still owning the cottage he and Annie had bought tucked away in the old part of town.

Lack of exercise over winter meant Sabine was panting by the time she pushed her key into the front-door lock. Still, the summer routine of walking into town and being on her feet for most of the day would soon have her fit again.

After organising supper for her and Johnnie – Peter was out with his girlfriend tonight – she made a mug of coffee and went upstairs to her studio. Her favourite place in the house.

Pressing a button on the CD player, Sabine sank down onto the settee and let the relaxing sounds of her favourite Miles Davis recording wash over her. Missy, her old tabby cat, immediately left the comfort of her basket in the alcove and sprang onto her lap.

A light and airy room courtesy of the dormer window she'd fought hard to get planning permission for, the room was exactly as she'd dreamt. A comfy two-seater settee with creamy loose covers over it and its feather-filled cushions, a bookcase down one wall holding her collection of art and teach yourself books, a wooden cabinet whose drawers and shelves held her paints, paper and other arty stuff as well as a combined radio and cd player. A small cane coffee table standing on a scarlet scatter rug on the wooden floorboards, polished and varnished to the nth degree by Johnnie, added a splash of colour to the room. An easel with her latest painting on it stood to one side of the dormer window and a few framed family photos were pinned to the ceiling beam that ran the width of the house. A small wood-burner on the side wall kept the room cosy in winter. Stacks of finished paintings were lined up wherever there was wall space.

Tristan at Churchside Gallery had offered to hang half a dozen or so of her paintings in a local artists' exhibition he was planning for May. For the last few months she'd been working on getting enough to sell over the season and to have some different ones to offer Tristan. It would be the first time her work had ever been hung in a proper gallery. Tristan had asked her to do some larger paintings of the river. 'Romanticise the scene,' he'd said. 'People can't get enough of pictures like that. An old boat or two is good – go for a nostalgic feel.'

Sabine had enjoyed painting the larger scenes and, as she'd grown more confident, she'd painted a couple of bright abstract ones, not knowing how Tristan would receive them. If he didn't want them, she'd give one to Johnnie and one to Owen.

Absently, Sabine stroked Missy. Normally in March she was full of energy and looking forward to the season. This year though, all the talk of the kiosk closing had unsettled her, making her question what the future might hold. And, if she were honest, made her feel old. Which was ridiculous. She still had plenty of years ahead of her. It was just a question of deciding how she was going to live them.

After all, her life so far had failed to be anything spectacular so that was unlikely to change. The one chance she'd had to change things had come at a wrong moment in her life. Now it was too late. The opportunity gone forever. Owen, at least, had never given up on her. Owen, apart from Johnnie, was the one person Sabine knew she could call in any emergency and know he'd be there for her. He would have made a wonderful father, she knew, from seeing him with Peter – she'd even deprived him of that. If only he'd met someone else, the pressure would have been off her, but no. Owen had proved steadfast in his love for her. Sabine remembered with gratitude Owen 'being there' for her and Peter through the years. He was a good man, still quite fit in his individual rugged way.

Sometimes, in the studio late at night when she felt lonely and vulnerable, she fantasised about accepting his proposal. Mrs Sabine Hutchinson had a good ring to it, but resolutely she always pushed the thought away. It wouldn't be fair to Owen.

Back down on the quay an hour later, she waited as the Queen of the River, with Peter at the helm, gently drew up alongside the pontoon.

Owen followed the last of the passengers up the pontoon gangway, leaving Peter and the other crew member to take the boat out to its mooring in the middle of the river.

'You got time for a quick drink?' he asked. 'Something we need to talk about.'

'Sounds serious,' Sabine said, her heart sinking. The beginning of the summer was not a good time for Owen to need to talk. 'Why not talk here?'

Owen shrugged. 'Rather sit in the pub in comfort. Besides, this way I get to enjoy your company for longer.'

'Have to be a quick one, Johnnie's coming for supper.'

'Won't take long what I've got to say,' Owen said. 'Ready?'

Ten minutes later, with a glass of chardonnay in front of her and a pint of beer in Owen's hand, Sabine looked at him. 'Well, what's this all about, Owen?'

'Will you marry me, Sabine?'

She shook her head. 'Sorry.'

'In that case, it's just two things. Peter and Hutchinson River Trips is the first.'

Sabine took a sip of her wine and waited. Was he regretting offering Peter a job and wanted out?

'I've been talking to the solicitor about Peter inheriting the business.'

It took a few seconds for his words to sink in.

'You want Peter to have the business? You're not ill, are you? You don't look ill but...'

'No I'm not ill,' Owen said.

'Thank god for that.'

'I just want to get things sorted and Peter's like the son I've never had to me.'

'Does Peter know about this?'

'Not yet. I wanted to make sure you didn't have any objections. Accuse me of forcing him to stay put before he's seen the world.'

'He's a real home bird,' Sabine said. 'I can't see him ever leaving for a life somewhere else. Besides, he loves his life on the river. But what about your dad's relatives? Surely there's a cousin or two out Stokenham way who have a claim to the family business?'

Owen shook his head. 'No. So what do you think? Good thing or not?'

'I think it's an incredibly generous action on your part, Owen,' Sabine said. 'But I hope he doesn't get to inherit too soon.'

'So do I, darling, so do I.' Owen laughed before taking a swig of his beer. 'Right, I'll get on to Trevor Bagshawe to do the necessary. Once that's done, we'll tell Peter, okay?'

Sabine nodded. 'You said there were two things – what's the second?'

'I've been talking to your Johnnie about all the places he's been. The sights he's seen. I've decided I've missed a lot so...'

'You're going to become a yacht deliverer?'

'No, of course not. At the end of the season I'm off touring Europe for six months.' Owen looked at her, a serious look on his face.

'Want to come with me? No strings. Just two old friends having an adventure together before it's too late.'

Chapter Two

Harriet

Harriet drew up outside The Captain's Berth with a sigh of relief. She'd made it. The longest drive she'd done on her own for years was finished. All four hours of it.

To say she'd been nervous when she set off this morning on her marathon journey was an understatement. She'd been close to tears and to forgetting the whole idea. She didn't have to put herself through the ordeal. She could wait for Frank to return from his unexpected meeting and travel down together like they'd planned. It was only by giving herself a severe talking-to, telling herself to stop being pathetic, that she was a grown woman for goodness sake, that she managed to get in the car. The first thirty miles had tested her willpower to keep going, but once she'd negotiated the traffic-filled motorway junction lanes outside Bristol, she relaxed. Familiar, long-forgotten landmarks began to mark the passage of miles and as she drove down the final miles to the Higher Ferry she smiled, glad she'd decided to come the scenic coastal route rather than inland.

Harriet fumbled for her keys and handbag before getting out of the car and making for the turquoise front door and raising the highly polished brass knocker.

'Hi. I'm Harriet Lewis. I've a room booked,' she said to the young woman who opened the door.

'Welcome to The Captain's Berth. I'm Angie. Let me help you with your luggage.'

Gratefully Harriet handed Angie the larger of the two cases before following her into the house and up the stairs.

'I've given you Room Two. It's the only double at the front with a view of the river. I hope you find it comfortable,' Angie said. 'Your husband?'

'Will be joining me later in the week,' Harriet said. 'Unexpected business trip.'

The room, light and airy, looked delightful to Harriet, its cream walls and carpeting a perfect foil for the vibrant floral bed linen and matching curtains. The bed, heaped with cushions, looked inviting and she couldn't wait to collapse onto it for a restorative nap.

'Tea and scones in ten minutes in the kitchen?' Angie said. 'Or would you prefer a tray up here?'

'Could I have a tray up here, please,' Harriet said, smiling at Angie whom she guessed was in her late twenties to early thirties – about the same age as Ellie, her daughter. 'I'm shattered after my long drive.' She didn't feel up to being sociable, answering any questions, one of which she knew would be along the lines of, 'First-time visitor to the town?'

'No problem. You've got tea-making facilities up here,' Angie said, pointing to the tray on the bedside table. 'I'll bring you some scones up.'

As Angie closed the door behind her, Harriet crossed to the window. The stretch of embankment and river visible to her encompassed the mouth of the river with its twin castles. Still early in the year, there was little activity on the water. The occasional sailing dinghy enjoying the breeze, a fishing trawler returning to harbour, men working on boats moored on the marina pontoons across the river. The few people strolling along the embankment disappeared from view as the road curved fractionally towards the Lower Ferry and rooftops blocked the view.

A discreet knock on the door as Angie returned with a tray laden with scones, jam and clotted cream. 'Enjoy. I'll see you later.'

Harriet switched the kettle on before starting to unpack. She hadn't brought a vast amount of clothes with her and the contents of the larger suitcase were hanging in the wardrobe before the kettle boiled. Unpacking the smaller weekend case could wait. Ten minutes later, sitting on the bentwood chair thoughtfully placed by a small table and enjoying her cream tea, Harriet tried to marshal her thoughts and plans into some sort of order.

She'd have a shower and then go for a walk, get some fresh air into her lungs.

The hot water hammering on her body as she stood under the powerful deluge of shower water, eyes closed, was therapeutic. Five minutes later, she stepped out, her tiredness banished. She'd resolved too, to stop thinking about Oscar and the past. Wrapping herself in the large, ultra-soft bath towel she took off the heated towel rail, Harriet picked up her phone.

She'd give Frank a quick text. If he was out of his meeting she knew he'd phone her back straight away.

Two minutes later, her phone beeped. 'You all right?' Frank asked.

'So far,' Harriet said. 'I haven't been out yet though.'

'I'll be there in two days. You could stay in the B&B until I get there if you want. Read a good book.'

'No, it will be fine. I'll be fine,' Harriet said. 'Have you heard from Ellie? I was thinking about ringing her.'

'Got a text to say she was busy at work, that's all. Don't worry, we'll talk to her together. Give her my love if you speak.'

'Will do. See you soon.' Harriet switched her phone over to messages and saw Ellie had sent her a text, as well, saying she was okay. Harriet sighed. Hopefully Frank was right, saying that Ellie would be fine when they talked to her. If only she hadn't had this dreadful sinking feeling in the pit of her stomach ever since she'd opened the letter last month. She should have struck through the address on the envelope, marked it 'Not known at this address – Return to Sender' and put it straight back in the post. Definitely not opened it.

The wording in the brief paragraph from a firm of solicitors had been innocuous in the extreme. Just a request for Harriet Lewis, formerly of Dartmouth, South Devon, to visit their offices in the town as soon as possible. And no, they weren't prepared to discuss the matter over the phone. When she showed the letter to Frank he immediately said they'd go down together, find out what it was all about, sort it and come home again.

'Whatever it is, darling, after all this time I'm sure it's nothing to worry about.'

Harriet had looked at him and tried to force herself to look at things dispassionately, re-reading again and again the brief letter, trying to work out if there was a hidden message in it anywhere. Her gut instinct was telling her that the letter was about to kick-start something nasty in her life. And tomorrow was the day she'd find out.

After pulling on her favourite jeans and a sweatshirt, Harriet grabbed her handbag and phone and went downstairs. Angie was playing with a Jack Russell in the conservatory attached to the kitchen.

'Oh he's gorgeous,' Harriet said, stopping down to stroke him. 'What's his name?'

'Solo,' Angie said. 'He likes to welcome all my guests. Are you off out?'

Harriet nodded. 'Thought I'd take a stroll around town.'

'Don't get lost!' Angie said. 'If you do, any local will point you in the right direction if you mention my name.'

'Thanks. I'll see you later.' No need to tell Angie there was very little likelihood of her getting lost. The town's ancient streets had once been a familiar backdrop to her life. If asked, she could have drawn a map.

Late afternoon and the bustle of the town was winding down for the day as Harriet began exploring. Stepping out from The Captain's Berth, with the river on her right, Harriet walked down towards the town. She hesitated by the steep flight of steps that led down to the fort situated at the end of the town's ancient quay before walking on. She'd go that route another day. Right now she wanted to wander around the town itself. Acclimatise herself to being here. Take in the changes that were sure to have happened. Re-acquaint herself with where things were within the town.

Wandering along the narrow old streets, many with medieval buildings still in use, Harriet realised while the town had retained its ancient layout, which was still second nature to her, there were subtle differences. Narrow streets were now either one way or pedestrianised, shops with modernised windows, selling touristy souvenirs. She certainly had no difficulty in finding her way to several places she remembered with nostalgia. Her old primary school was still there but converted into flats. The old cinema had gone though, replaced with a modern complex complete with a new library alongside.

She spent time window shopping in the boutiques in the converted Old Palladium Mews before skirting around the church, climbing a well-worn flight of steps and finding herself at the junction of the steep hill that led eventually out of town to join the coast road and, to the left, the narrow road that wound its way behind the houses on the main town road. No way was she going to walk in that direction today. It was too soon, best left for another day. Harriet turned and made her way down to the quay where, judging by the smell wafting around and accompanying loudly squawking seagulls, the local fishing boats were unloading their day's catch of crabs and mackerel.

Watching the plastic crates being swung onto the quayside before being loaded into the pick-up truck ready for delivery to various local restaurants, Harriet looked curiously at the fishermen on board one of the boats. One was about her own age, the other younger. Was the older man a part of her past? An old school friend, maybe? A long-forgotten memory of a secret crush trickled into her mind. Gus was the son of a fisherman. But Gus, as a teenager, had vowed no way was he following in the fishy footsteps of his father and grandfather. There had to be more to life, he maintained, and he intended to explore its full potential.

The younger of the fishermen smiled at Harriet as he caught her watching them. Harriet smiled back before moving away and wandering in the direction of the inner harbour. Passing the brightly painted closed ticket kiosk, Harriet smiled, remembering the summer she and her best friend Beeny had hung around there for hours longing to be noticed by the Rod

Stewart lookalike employed to sell trips up the river to the tourists.

Another teenage memory from a long-ago summer flitted into her mind as she saw a tourist boat slowly making its way back down river. An illicit June evening trip up river, creeping on board with Beeny without buying a ticket, hoping bad-tempered Mitch Hutchinson wouldn't notice them and have them thrown off. Beeny French-kissed Owen, his son, for his silence when he found them and realised they hadn't paid. Funny how it was only Beeny he'd wanted to kiss. She hadn't cared, though. The only person she was interested in kissing in those days was Gus. Not that she had, of course. She'd been invisible to him.

Harriet glanced at a blackboard nailed to the side of the kiosk with neat chalk-writing advertising the times of the next trips up the river. Gold lettering at the top proclaimed: 'Hutchinson River Trips. Established 1931.' Was Owen running the family business now? Did Beeny still live in town? Funny how the old kiosk was kick-starting so many memories. Turning, she crossed the road and walked towards the Royal Avenue Gardens.

Standing by the inner harbour, its muddy waters crammed with boats small enough to pass under the embankment bridge to reach the river, her stomach rumbled and she realised she was ravenous, Angie's delicious scones not enough to make up for her missed lunch. She glanced behind her at The Royal Castle Hotel. Time for more nostalgia. Turning, she crossed the road and made her way into the hotel foyer, automatically turning right for the bar and restaurant.

After ordering a steak salad, Harriet took her glass of wine over to a window table and settled down to wait for her meal. Looking around, she could see the place had been extensively modernised since the last time she'd been there, but had somehow managed to retain most of its atmosphere from the eighteenth-century days when it had been a busy coaching inn.

'Enjoy your meal,' the waitress said, smiling at her. As she heard the Birmingham accent, Harriet smiled back. An incomer. Not a possible old friend from a past life. Good. She wasn't ready to meet any of those yet.

Glancing around at the other people in the restaurant, an elderly couple, a family of six with an adorable toddler, a group of locals having a drink at the end of the working day, Harriet pushed her self-conscious feelings of being conspicuously alone away. She'd always hated dining alone. At least it wasn't a permanent state of affairs. Frank would be joining her in two days. Tomorrow she would buy a book to read as she ate. Tonight she'd people watch and make plans for tomorrow and the meeting with Trevor Bagshawe, solicitor, to which she and Frank had planned to go together but now she was having to face alone.

Chapter Three

Johnnie

Johnnie whistled tunelessly as he steered Annie on a falling tide across the Dart towards the grid. He loved the river at this time of day. Early evening and the light of the day was disappearing, although there was still activity on the water.

The Higher Ferry, its three lanes crammed with cars full of returning commuters from work in Torquay or even Exeter, was making its way across to the Dartmouth slipway. The naval college lorded it over Sandquay and the marina in the deepening gloom. Motoring past one of the huge black buoys in the middle of the river, he watched a shag preening itself, perched on the iron ring while seagulls wheeled and screeched overhead. When one wheeled directly over his head, aiming for Annie's mast, Johnnie shouted 'Bugger off', knowing it was a useless shout. He'd waged a constant vendetta against them for years to Sabine's amusement.

'They're part of the river's landscape,' she always said.

'Bloody vermin,' he'd mutter back.

Further up river, on the banks that were appearing as the tide went out, oyster catchers were busy prodding around in the mud. He'd timed his arrival at the maintenance grid perfectly and, once Annie was alongside the embankment wall, he cut the engine.

'Throw me the rope and I'll tie you up aft,' a female voice said.

'Thanks.' And he threw the stern line up towards the woman who expertly caught it and began to tie it to one of the rings. Johnnie went forward to the bow and threw the mooring rope curled up on the deck onto the quay before stepping off the boat onto the landing ladder and climbing up to the embankment.

'Nice boat,' the woman said.

'Thanks,' Johnnie answered, concentrating on pulling the bow into the position he needed for Annie to settle properly on the grid overnight. Once he was satisfied, he turned his attention to the stern rope, but the woman had done a good job there, releasing and tightening the rope as necessary whilst he did the bow.

'Done a bit of sailing, then?' he said. She might be wearing an expensive yachting waterproof jacket, but that was no guarantee she'd ever stepped on board a boat. Some women wore nautical clothes to be fashionable when around boats and water. Although Johnny had to admit she'd done a pretty proficient job with the rope.

'Just a bit.' The woman smiled at him. 'Have a good evening.'

'You too.'

Johnnie watched as she walked away. Nice smile. He couldn't remember seeing her around the river before, and he knew he'd remember that smile, so he'd guess she was a holidaymaker.

He stayed on board Annie for half an hour, adjusting the ropes as she settled down on the grid, the wooden piles against the embankment wall keeping her off the stones. Once he was happy with the way she was settling, he grabbed his laptop from the chart table, secured the cockpit hatch and set off for Sabine's and supper. Ten minutes later, he was sitting in her cosy kitchen.

'You all right?' he asked as she placed the chicken casserole on the table. 'You're a bit quiet tonight.'

Sabine shrugged. 'Things on my mind.'

Johnnie knew better than to probe. Sabine would tell him in her own time.

'Took a booking this afternoon for a delivery over to St. Malo next week,' he said. 'Forty-foot motor yacht so should be a quick trip. Only be away for three or four days at the most. Be back for Easter.'

'Good. Did you get Annie across ready for tomorrow?'

Johnnie nodded. 'Yep.'

'You want to sleep here tonight?' Sabine asked, knowing the yacht would be at an uncomfortable angle once the tide was fully out.

'Thanks, but I'll go to the cottage.' He shrugged as Sabine glanced at him. 'Needs an airing.'

'Got a few signatures on the kiosk petition this afternoon by the way,' Sabine said before adding, 'Owen is planning on leaving Peter his boat business.'

'Strewth. Bloody generous of him,' Johnnie said. 'Any strings?' Given how fond he knew Owen was of his sister, maybe it was a ruse to gain her love? No. Not Owen's style at all.

Sabine shook her head. 'No. He just thinks of Peter as the son he never had.'

'Set Peter up that's for sure,' Johnnie said. 'What does he say?'

'Doesn't know yet. Owen is getting it all formalised before he tells him.'

Sabine stood up and cleared the plates away before placing an apple tart and a dish of clotted cream on the table in front of Johnnie.

'Help yourself. Had my first American of the season book a ticket today. And guess what? He's researching his family history! *Quelle surprise*! Why can't they leave the past alone? Asked me if I knew any Holdsworths.'

'What did you say?'

'Basically that, unlike small-town America, I knew the name but I don't know everybody in the town.'

'Pretty sure there aren't any living in the town now,' Johnnie said. 'Didn't we go to school with a girl who had Holdsworth relatives, though?'

'She was the one I wanted you to marry so we could be sisters,' Sabine said. 'Wonder if he's going to turn out to be related to that branch of the family.'

'You ever hear what happened to your friend?'

Sabine shook her head. 'Nope. Family simply vanished at the height of the scandal.'

On his way home later that evening, Johnnie stopped by the yacht to check everything was okay before crossing the embankment road and making for Undercliffe. The cottage he and Annie had bought when they married, filled with youthful optimism, no longer felt like home without her there. It had lost the wonderful homely and safe feeling that Annie had created within its walls. Now it was just a cottage where many painful memories blocked out the happy ones. He needed a drink to stay in the place these days.

Picking up the post from the doormat, he rifled through it. A letter from France, caught up in between the pamphlets and newspapers of junk mail that his post mainly consisted of these days, he placed on the table. He recognised Cousin Martha's writing. Daughter of

Tante Brigitte, his father's younger sister, she was the one who kept him and Sabine up to date with family news these days. She was also the one whom he'd stayed with during those first dreadful days after he'd lost Annie and he'd fled to France.

Pouring himself a finger of whisky and taking the letter, he wandered through into the small sitting room and sank down onto the leather Chesterfield. Thank god his drinking was under control, thanks to Sabine, but he knew she would still have taken the bottle of whisky he'd hidden under the kitchen sink away if she'd realised it was there. 'Too much temptation,' she'd say.

Carefully he opened the letter. Bound to have lots of family news – there was still quite a large contingent of LeRoys in the small town his father had been born in. As he'd thought, the letter was full of news about the younger generation not doing well at school, the state of fishing was terrible and the new prime minister didn't have a clue and when was he coming over? It would be a good idea if he came soon – but there was no reason given. Normally Brigitte simply said: 'Looking forward to seeing you sometime soon', but this: 'It would be a good idea to come soon' sounded more like an order. Was something up? Did they need his advice or was it a typically French reaction to something minor? Well it wouldn't be until after Easter, that was for sure. A couple of deliveries were lined up – one to Spain and one to the west coast of Ireland. He'd give her a ring later. Find out what the problem was exactly. He took a slug of his whisky, savouring the warmth as he swallowed. Closing his eyes, he leant back against the settee.

Annie had loved the whole cottage, but this room had been her favourite to sit in and read. Johnnie could still see her curled up, lost to the world as she read the latest bestseller. Part of him knew the sensible thing would be to sell the place. He rarely spent a night here these days, preferring to be out on the boat.

He should buy another place without the memories. Or even a bigger boat. Move on like Sabine had when Dave died. Buying the cottage after the trauma of Dave being lost at sea, had certainly helped Sabine to get her life back on track. Strange really how they'd both lost their partners so early in life, but he'd always felt that while Annie had been the love of his life, Sabine hadn't loved Dave in the same way. Oh they'd loved each other for sure, but he wasn't convinced that they'd been true soul mates like him and Annie. Sabine had deserved a second chance with someone, but sadly it had never happened.

A voice in his head asked how could he bear to sever the tenacious connection the cottage provided with Annie. The simple answer was: he couldn't. Not yet. Maybe at the end of summer he'd think about it.

Chapter Four

Rachel

Rachel stood back and looked at the cake critically. Cake decorating had never been high on her list of 'learn how to do' skills. In the past it had been so easy to nip down to the local patisserie and buy their most highly decorated concoction whenever she'd been asked to provide a cake. Somehow, even if that option was still available, she doubted that approach would go down well with the organisers of this particular fund-raising event who'd asked her to donate a cake. Every one of them was sure to be a closet Mary Berry.

So this chocolate-covered three-tiered sponge had to be as good as she could make it. No doubt it's homemade appearance would lose her brownie points and its butter-cream icing would be found wanting, but so be it.

Rachel smiled wryly to herself as she carefully placed the cake in the largest box she could find, ready to deliver it later that morning. Who'd have thought, six months ago, she'd be baking a cake and participating in a spot of charity work? Not her, for sure. When she'd arrived, still stunned by the changes in her life, she'd simply wanted to shut herself away. Which she did. The only person she'd spoken to on a regular basis was

Hugo, who phoned her daily, telling her she should never have left France and begging her to return to the villa. The one thing Rachel was determined not to do. At least not permanently, maybe a holiday in due course to see everyone would be wonderful. But first she had to sort her life out.

Avoiding face-to-face contact with people, for weeks she ordered her food over the Internet for home delivery on a Friday with the instructions to leave the box in the porch. It had taken two months for her to discover she wasn't cut out to be a hermit and to start craving some sort of social life. When she told Hugo she was starting to go out, his sigh of relief was audible down the phone. Within weeks she'd joined the library, been roped in to help at the town's charity shop, found a favourite place for coffee and been cajoled into joining a book club which was where, after several glasses of wine following a particularly boring discussion, Susannah and Caroline had extracted a promise from her to bake a cake for their next coffee morning. And so far nobody had questioned her too closely about her past.

Her 'I've lived abroad for years' reply when asked about where she'd previously lived, quickly followed by 'My husband died recently' earned her sympathetic looks and stopped people probing too deep. Although there had been a moment just last week at the book club when Caroline had pursed her lips and said: 'Where are you from originally? I've been trying to place your accent but can't quite make it out.' To Rachel's relief, before she could answer, somebody called out for more wine and Caroline had moved away.

Glancing out of the kitchen window, she saw a sailing boat beating its way up river and for a moment she longed to be out there on board. Sailing was definitely on her agenda for this summer. She'd ask Susannah at the coffee morning later if she knew anybody who wanted the occasional crew. Maybe she'd brave the sailing club too and ask there.

Moving into the sitting room, with its large patio doors opening onto the terrace, it struck her how at home she was beginning to feel in the house. Something she hadn't expected to feel in such a short time. But here were no memories lurking in every room to pull her up, to remind her how different her life had been just a few short months ago. Coming back was looking increasingly like it had been the right decision. She was living life on her own terms. For the first time in months she realised she was … not happy exactly, more like content.

The coffee morning was already in full swing in the charity shop when Rachel arrived. She pushed her way carefully through the crowd to the small cafe area and put her cake on the table. As she'd feared, placed next to a plate of expertly decorated cupcakes and a professional-looking carrot cake with a frosted topping, her chocolate cake did indeed look amateurish.

'Hi, thanks for this,' Susannah said, immediately cutting it into slices. 'People always go for chocolate – especially the ones that look so obviously homemade. Are you okay to stay and help for a while? Could do with a hand feeding the hordes.'

'Sure,' Rachel said. Half an hour later, as things started to quieten down, she was pleased to see only a single slice of chocolate cake left. Couldn't have been that bad then. Pouring herself a cup of coffee, she stood back and looked around.

She already recognised one or two faces. The lady from the library, the girl from the post office, even the traffic warden had popped in for a quick coffee. Two elderly ladies were talking quietly together as they browsed the book section. Parts of their conversation drifted over to Rachel.

'Sad she had to die in the nursing home. Can't help wondering what's going on with her estate now though.'

'Didn't have any relatives, did she?'

'A twin brother. Not that he visited much, even when she was ill. They fell out years ago. Think he died recently too.'

'Maybe she left all her money to charity.'

'Wouldn't be surprised. She always was a close one. Wouldn't mind her house. If it comes on the market, might go and take a look. Got wonderful views. Bet it'll be expensive though, nothing ever comes cheap in Swannaton. Oh look what I've found, an Erica James. Have to buy it. Love her books.' And the two women moved away.

Rachel's hand shook as she replaced her coffee cup on the table. Was the woman they were talking about the one person she'd dreaded bumping into ever since she'd arrived here? Guiltily Rachel hoped it was. It would mean there was no chance of them meeting unexpectedly. It couldn't just be coincidence. How many women living in Swannaton had a recently deceased twin brother?

The final link in town to her past would have been severed. With no-one left to drag them out of her cupboard and dangle them in front of her, her skeletons could finally be laid to rest.

Chapter Five

Ellie

The day Ellie Lewis was made redundant from her job as features editor with a famous women's magazine turned out to be the day her relationship with Rod Vicars also fell apart. Ellie berated herself for weeks for not seeing either event coming.

She'd known, of course, about the redundancies sweeping through the industry, but had stupidly assumed her job was safe. Even consoled her friend Sally with the words, 'Think of it as a new opportunity' when she'd received the dreaded summons. Now she had her own unwanted new opportunity to deal with.

Andy, the editor, had been apologetic as he'd given her the news, saying he'd tried to save her job but 'upstairs' had refused. 'Given you a generous package though,' he'd added. As if that made all the difference. She needed to work.

Clearing her desk and packing up her personal stuff in the box thoughtfully provided alongside her redundancy notice took five minutes in the strangely quiet office with everybody conspicuously studying their screens rather than look at her.

'I'm not bloody contagious,' she muttered. But maybe redundancy was?

Estelle, the fashion editor, late to work as usual, took in the scene instantly when she arrived.

'Oh, honey, I'm so sorry,' she said, enveloping Ellie in a hug. 'What a shock. You all right?' She held Ellie at arm's-length and studied her critically. 'Take a few days holiday, get Rod to spoil you. You'll bounce back. Give me a ring next week – we'll have lunch.'

'Thanks, Estelle. Would you like this?' Ellie held out the orchid plant that had sat on her desk all year without a single flower. 'You might have more luck with it than me.'

She picked up the box and her laptop and called out, 'Bye, everyone. Good luck!' before walking out of the office without a backward glance.

Ellie decided to walk home via the park rather than take the bus. The box wasn't heavy and her laptop bag was comfy across her shoulder. After all, there was nothing to rush for and the sun was shining. The takeaway chalet near the lake was open and she treated herself to a Danish pastry and a coffee. Necessary comfort food.

Sitting on a wooden bench and watching mums and their children feed the ducks, Ellie started to think things through. Ever practical, she counted the plusses currently in her life. One, she had a roof over her head. Two, she was in a loving relationship. Although that had been a bit strained recently with them both being so busy. A short time off work would give her the opportunity to spoil Rod. She'd start by cooking his favourite meal tonight – coq au vin. Maybe he'd open one of his special red wines that he kept in a box under his bed. They could at least drink to the future. Once she'd dumped her stuff off at home, she'd do a supermarket shop and stock the cupboards. Three, the redundancy cheque was enough to live on for at least three months – even taking into account her share of the high rent for their serviced flat.

Right, that was the pros taken care of. Now for the cons. One, she was unemployed. Two, there weren't a lot of jobs around at the moment. Three, she couldn't actually think of a third. The first two were bad enough. What if she didn't get a job for months and months? Would Rod even consider moving to a non-serviced flat where he actually had to do something like take the rubbish to the bin rather than just put the black bag outside the door for the caretaker to pick up? Unlikely.

He'd lived in the modern, minimalistic flat for two years now. Ellie had moved in with him just six months ago at his suggestion. At first she'd tried to add some of her own touches – a scarlet throw over the settee to bring some colour into the black-and-white decor, a picture or two but Rod hated them. The only things he tolerated were her candles and two scarlet cushions – and then only when she protested it was her home too.

Even with her contributing to the rent, he moaned every month about the extortionate charges. Somehow she couldn't see him agreeing to give up the apartment and rent a cheaper one because she'd lost her job and couldn't afford to contribute. As far as he was concerned, his address was a status symbol. On the other hand, he might wave his hand airily, tell her not to worry, he'd look after her – and pick the rent up. Ellie sighed. Rod never had been one with the expansive gestures.

Ellie finished the pastry and threw the remains of the cold coffee on the grass. She'd have the rest of the week off and then next week she'd refresh her CV and start job-hunting in earnest. Maybe register with an agency for some temp work. See if there were any freelancing opportunities around.

Rod was in the sitting room, tapping hard on his laptop when she got home.

'I didn't realise you were working from home today,' she said.

'Have to see a client round the corner in ...' He glanced at his watch. 'Hell, in five minutes. Got to go.'

He snapped his laptop shut, glanced at his phone and was halfway out of the door before asking, 'What are you doing home anyway?'

Ellie shrugged. Now was not the right moment to break the bad redundancy news. 'Tell you later. Hope they sign on the dotted line.'

'Thanks. See you about six then.'

But it was gone seven when Rod arrived home that evening. Ellie had set the table, lit a couple of candles and generally tried to make the apartment as cosy as she could for an intimate dinner before she told Rod about losing her job. The coq au vin, though, was in danger of becoming dehydrated despite the extra half-bottle of merlot she'd poured over it.

Ellie took one look at Rod's face as he saw the table and the candles and knew there was something wrong.

'This is a bit OTT for a Monday evening, isn't it? We celebrating something?' he asked.

'No. I just had time today so I thought I'd spoil us both with a nice dinner. It's been ages since we had an evening like this,' Ellie said, handing him a glass of wine. As they chinked glasses, she said, 'Not since the first month of me moving into the flat really. We've both been too busy.'

'And today you're not?'

'No. I'm redundant,' Ellie said, wishing she'd waited a bit longer before announcing it so bluntly, but the words had come out of her mouth of their own accord.

'Ah. Well I've got some job news too.'

'Oh god – you're not redundant too?' If he was, the flat would definitely have to go. No way could they afford to keep it on. 'What are we going to do?'

'I've been promoted to Branch Manager.'

'Oh that's brilliant,' Ellie said, raising her glass in a toast. Judging by the long hours Rod had been putting in recently, she'd guessed the housing market was picking up. The prestigious estate agency he worked for must have realised how good he was at selling houses. At least he'd be earning more money while she found another job. 'Which branch?'

'Manchester.'

'Where?'

'Manchester.'

Ellie waved her hand in disbelief. 'I heard you the first time.' She picked up the merlot bottle and topped up her glass. 'When did this all kick off?'

'Couple of weeks ago. Nothing definite until this week.'

'Why didn't you tell me before?'

'No point until I knew for definite.'

'When do you start?'

'First of the month.'

'That's less than a fortnight away.'

Rod nodded. 'Yep. Lot of things to sort before then.'

'But I don't want to live in Manchester.' Ellie took a drink of her wine as the silence between them lengthened.

'You're not coming,' Rod said flatly. 'You just have to move out of here.'

'What?'

'You couldn't afford the rent without me even if you were working. Now you're redundant...' Rod shrugged.

'But what about us? Are we breaking up because you're moving to Manchester? Or were you taking the opportunity to break up with me?'

Rod's silence and the look on his face confirmed Ellie had hit on the truth with her last question.

'Why didn't you tell me straight? I thought you loved me? We could have talked – still can.'

This time Rod did answer her. 'No point. I've met someone else who is coming to Manchester with me.'

Chapter Six

BB

Being a sociable kind of man, when Braxton Brael saw the woman from the kiosk and the captain of the Queen of the River in the hotel bar when he walked in, he didn't hesitate to stroll over and say, 'Hi. Can I buy you guys a drink?'

Sabine shook her head and smiled at him. 'Not for me, thanks. Got things to do when I get home. Too many glasses of wine and I'll be asleep.'

'Half a lager for me would be very nice of you,' Owen said.

Braxton turned to the barman and ordered two lagers. 'There you go, Skipper. Have to tell you how much I enjoyed my jaunt up the river. Learnt a lot from your commentary.'

'Discovered any relations yet?' Sabine asked.

Braxton shook his head. 'Nope not yet, ma'am, but I'm working on it. Got a couple of other things to sort out as well.' He extended his hand to her. 'Guess I'd better introduce myself. I'm Braxton Brael – known as BB to my friends.'

'Hello, BB. I'm Sabine and this is Owen.'

'You in town for long?' Owen asked.

'Planning on staying for summer. Looking to rent an apartment, buy a boat and find those relatives!'

'What sort of boat?' Owen asked.

'I'm pretty flexible on that score but a forty-foot wooden sailing ketch would fit the bill perfectly,' BB said. 'I'll just have to see what turns up during summer.'

'You planning on sailing back to America?'

'Sure am. Will need a crew, of course, but first I've got to find the boat. Would sure appreciate any contacts you could give me.'

'You need to talk to my brother Johnnie,' Sabine said, getting down from her bar stool. 'He's a yacht deliverer. Gets a lot of work from various agencies. He'll know if there are any suitable boats around. I'll mention you to him. Right, got to go. Thanks for the drink, Owen, see you tomorrow. Nice to meet you properly, BB. Good luck with all your searches. See you around.'

'Appreciate that,' BB said, turning to Owen as Sabine left. 'Nice lady.'

Owen nodded. 'One of the best. I'm afraid I'm off too. Can I refill that for you before I go?' he asked, looking at the glass in BB's hand.

'No thanks. I'm on my way into the restaurant for dinner,' BB said lifting the glass to his lips and finishing his drink before making his way through to the restaurant.

After dinner, BB handed his room key to the receptionist in the foyer and went out. A walk around town before bed would be good. He stood for a few moments, deciding which way to go before crossing the road. The tide was coming in and the small boats in the inner harbour, moored closely together, were nudging fenders as the water shifted them. The evening air was cool and the gusts of wind making the river choppy had him zipping up his fleece and pulling the collar higher as he crossed the road to the embankment, turning in the direction of the Higher Ferry.

Bit late this evening to explore the marina at this end of town he'd glimpsed on his river trip, but at least he'd be able to check if there was a yachting agency he could register with. Glancing up at the Royal Naval College, sitting on the hill dominating the town, the silver-framed photo of Grandpa Millman aged nineteen and his brother, Uncle Lance, twenty-one, that stood on the bureau in his mother's bedroom came into his mind. Taken before they'd left for Europe, both stood tall and proud in their GI uniforms, arms around each other's shoulders. So sad that Lance hadn't survived the war, Grandpa Millman had always spoken of his big brother with affection and admitted he still missed him. Had either of them ever been inside that wonderful building? Or had they spent all their time out in one of the field camps?

After locating the yachting agency and checking opening hours, BB turned and walked back to the hotel. He'd promised to Skype Jessica this evening at ten o'clock his time.

Jessica was already online when he opened his laptop and signed in.

'Hi, Bro! How's it going? Found us any wealthy cousins yet?'

'Barely started really, Jess but it's great here. You'd love it. No sign of any cousins yet – wealthy or otherwise.'

'Shame. You have, of course, taken some photos?'

'Yep. I'll email them tomorrow. How's Mom?'

'She's okay-ish. She's finally started to go through the last of Grandmother Mary's boxes of papers.'

'Must be hard for her. Found anything interesting?'

'Not yet. Lots of letters from both Grandpa Randy and Uncle Lance and a few other bits, but we have unearthed a box of stuff that appears to be from WWII. I'm going to go through that as soon as I have a moment. Feel a bit guilty – it's a bit like reading someone's private diary but it's fascinating.'

'All in the name of research. You haven't found any papers about Grandmother Mary's own background?'

'Nope. Hoping you'll have more luck now you're over there.'

'Fingers crossed. Give my love to Mom. I'll let you know as soon as I discover anything, but right now I'm off to bed to do a little night-time reading about Dartmouth.'

'And I've got to pick up the kids from school. Night.'

BB closed his laptop before moving across to the window. From his vantage point on the fourth floor, he could see the lights on the river and across on the opposite bank. What was that place? Ah, Kingswear. So many places to explore/visit, but tomorrow he was going to concentrate on finding somewhere to live for summer.

Chapter Seven

Harriet

'So there you have it, Mrs Lewis. You inherit your ex-sister-in-law's house here in town and your daughter inherits a substantial sum of money from a trust set up by her aunt which I will have to talk to her about personally – provided you accept the legacy and the conditions attached to it.'

'How substantial a sum?' Harriet asked weakly. 'And the conditions?'

Trevor Bagshawe rustled a few papers before looking up and saying, 'As of yesterday, £900,000. But, of course, there is interest accruing all the time.'

Nine hundred thousand pounds? How the hell had Amy accumulated that kind of money? It wasn't an amount she, Harriet, could even dream of recompensing Ellie with when she turned down the legacy. Which she would. No way could she accept whatever the conditions were. The impact on Ellie's life would be too colossal.

'There are just two conditions, both quite brief and to the point,' Trevor said and started to read from one of the pieces of paper. 'One. You must agree to live in the house for at least a year and keep it in good repair. Two. Ellie must eventually inherit it. In other words,' he glanced up at Harriet, 'you are not allowed to sell it. There is a sum of money entailed with the house to pay for essential maintenance.'

He placed the papers down on his desk and smiled at her. 'So nothing too contentious there. Your sister-in-law also left you a private letter.' He pushed a sealed envelope across the desk towards her.

Harriet could only look at him in dismay. Nothing contentious? What did he know? The first condition rendered everything unacceptable.

'Has your firm acted for Amy in other matters?' Harriet asked, fingering the embossed envelope. Just how much did this man know about her and the scandal that had torn her life apart years ago?

'Oh yes,' Trevor said. 'Not me personally. I only joined the firm two years ago, but I understand Mr Atkins, the senior partner, was a great friend and had advised Miss Widdicombe for a number of years on various matters. I took over most of his probate cases when he retired last year.'

'I see.' Did that mean he knew the history behind this bequest? No way was she going to ask the question.

'It's a small town, Mrs Lewis, but confidentiality is everything in our business,' the solicitor said quietly, somehow sensing her unspoken question.

So he did know about her past. No secrets in small towns, however hard you try. Harriet could imagine the tittle-tattle that would happen once the locals, particular the older ones, realised who had inherited Amy Widdicombe's house.

'I have to think about this. Talk to my husband. To my daughter,' Harriet said. 'It's a bit of a shock.'

Trevor nodded. 'Understandable. I have a key to the house if you'd like to take a look?'

'Umm,' Harriet hesitated. 'Okay. Thanks,' she said, standing up. Easier to take the key than to make an excuse. Right now, she needed some air and space to think.

'One more thing, Mrs Lewis,' Trevor said. 'If for some reason you decide not to accept the legacy conditions, our instructions are to sell the house and donate the money to a local charity – along with the monies from the trust fund.'

So Ellie would end up with nothing. Would never need to know about Amy or her brother. The whole episode could stay in the past and Ellie could continue to live her life in happy ignorance.

Harriet, left the solicitor's office and made her way through town with no real knowledge of where she was going, but instinctively making for the remembered back lanes, away from the shops and people until she found herself walking through the Royal Avenue Gardens and crossing the road towards the embankment.

Why, oh why, had Amy left her and Ellie the house? No contact for years and now a bequest that threatened everything she held dear. How was Frank – let alone Ellie – going to react to this legacy from her past?

A few people were strolling along the embankment, enjoying the afternoon sunshine and watching the activity on the river. Harriet dodged around a young couple lost in a world of their own. Ahead of her she could see four or five people standing by the river trips kiosk, eating hot cross buns, drinking coffee and generally blocking the way. Harriet, quickly glancing behind her to check the traffic, stepped off the pavement and crossed the road, not wanting to disturb what was clearly a friendly get-together amongst locals.

Wandering up Newcomen Road and into South Town, Harriet could feel the key in her pocket banging against her leg. Amy's house was just up the road. She could walk there in less than ten minutes if she wanted to. Maybe she'd just go and look at the outside. Looking wouldn't affect her decision in any way. But why bother to even look at the house – it would only bring back painful memories – when she had no intention of accepting the legacy. Knowing Frank though, he would insist on exploring every eventuality, every possible escape clause, before he'd allow her to turn the offer down.

Deep in thought, Harriet walked on, barely noticing her surroundings until she reached the junction of Swannaton and Above Town. Decision time. Fingering the key in her pocket, she stood looking up at the short steep incline that was the beginning of Swannaton. How many times in the past had she breathlessly pushed Ellie in her stroller up there to reach Aunt Amy's house a hundred yards or so further on from where she stood now? Did she want to re-trace those footsteps today? On her own? Without the support of Frank? So many memories would surface. Memories that were hers alone – her life before Frank. It would be better to face them privately. But not today, Harriet decided, turning resolutely on to the Above Town road. The implications of the legacy were enough to think about for now, without adding sentimental nostalgia into the mix. Easier to think straight, plan how she was going to convince Frank that refusing to accept Amy's inheritance was the right thing to do, without the complication of remembering how happy she'd once been when the house had been a part of her life.

Walking back into town along the narrow road, Harriet tried to marshal her thoughts into a logical order, the way she'd point them out to Frank. The main stipulation of the legacy that she must live in the house for a year would be the real deal-breaker with Frank, she was sure. No way would he countenance giving up his own home, even temporarily. It was too convenient for work, the golf club and, after twenty years, he'd finally got the garden the way he wanted.

Harriet took a deep breath as she approached the Crowthers Hill junction. Who was she trying to kid that, so long as Frank agreed with refusing the legacy, everything would be fine. Deep down, she knew it was really Ellie, the daughter she'd give her life for, who was at the root of the biggest moral and guilt-induced headache that was beginning to throb in her head.

'Good god! I don't believe it. Tatty?' A woman running down to the junction stopped and stared in amazement at her.

Harriet, herself forced to stop to avoid bumping into the woman, looked at her equally surprised.

'Beeny?'

'Yes.' The woman threw her arms around Harriet and hugged her. 'God, it's so good to see you.'

'You too,' Harriet said, returning the hug.

'Are you on holiday? We must meet. Catch up.'

'Lots of catching up to do,' Harriet said ruefully.

'Come to supper tonight. Six doors up on the right. Scarlet front door. Seven o'clock.'

Harriet hesitated before smiling and saying 'Just you and me? Okay. But please don't mention to anyone that you've bumped into me.'

'Promise. Have to dash, I'm already late,' Sabine said. 'See you later.'

'Look forward to it,' Harriet said as Sabine waved and ran on down the hill.

Chapter Eight

Sabine / Harriet

Late afternoon and Sabine was closing up the kiosk when Owen arrived.

'Any chance of a coffee? Been checking the moorings and boy is it cold out on the river. I'm in desperate need of a warm drink.'

'You'll have to make it yourself and finish locking up for me,' Sabine said. 'Need to get home early tonight.'

'Doing something special?'

'Just supper with a friend,' Sabine said.

'Anyone I know?'

Sabine shook her head. 'Sorry, I've been sworn to secrecy. See you tomorrow.'

Walking home, Sabine wondered why Harriet had made her promise not to tell anyone she was back in town. She must realise no-one would give a tinker's cuss these days about the past scandal. Too many present-day ones to gossip about. Besides, the town was full of incomers nowadays, who had no idea what had happened thirty years ago.

Harriet, as Sabine had known she would be, was early.

'Still, "Mrs Can't Bear to be Late", then?' she teased as she led the way up to the studio. Harriet's obsession with getting to places early and hers for never being on time anywhere, had always been a joke between them.

'Judging by the way you were running when we met earlier, I bet you still get to places late more often than on time,' Harriet said.

Sabine laughed. 'True.'

'Oh what a lovely room,' Harriet said as she walked into the studio. 'Are these paintings yours? Is that what you are into these days?'

Sabine nodded. 'Spend all my free time painting. Got my first exhibition coming up in May.'

'Brilliant! What time will Dave be home?' Harriet asked. 'I can't wait to see him again.'

Sabine stilled before saying quietly. 'Dave died. Fourteen years ago.'

'Beeny, I'm so sorry. I didn't know.'

'Amy didn't tell you?'

'You weren't the only one I lost contact with when I left,' Harriet said quietly. 'There's been a thirty-year moratorium on news from here.'

Sabine looked at her. 'Oh, Tatty. That's so sad.'

'No-one's called me Tatty in all that time,' Harriet said.

'Drink. We need a drink,' Sabine said. 'I'll be back in two ticks. Then I'll attempt to fill you in with things.'

Harriet was looking at the photos pinned to the beams when Sabine returned with wine and some nibbles.

'You have a son?' she asked, pointing to one of Sabine cuddling a toddler.

'Yep that's Peter. Twenty now.'

'Ten years younger than Ellie then.'

'How is Ellie? Can't believe that cute toddler bridesmaid at my wedding is all grown up.'

'She's fine. Trained as a journalist and works for one of the large media companies. She's not married but lives with Rod.' Harriet pulled a face. 'We feel sure she could do better than him but, hey, when did any of us ever choose the partner our parents wanted?'

'We?'

'Frank, my husband. He adopted Ellie when she was three. Loves her to bits.'

Harriet took the glass of wine Sabine had poured her. 'Have you re-married?'

Sabine shook her head. 'No. Owen keeps asking me but ...' she shrugged.

'Owen as in Owen Hutchinson?'

'That's the one. I work for him these days, managing the booking kiosk on the quay for river trips.'

'I passed there earlier this morning. Didn't see you – there were lots of people drinking coffee and eating buns.'

'Impromptu meeting of the Save the Kiosk group. Council want to do away with it,' Sabine said. 'Make us use an office somewhere else on the quay.' She took a sip of wine. 'So, catch-up time. Papa died shortly after you left. Johnnie is a widower. His Annie died two years ago. Owen's never married but regards Peter as his son. Gus is back from making his fortune.'

'And did he?' Harriet asked.

'Seems like it. Something to do with computers that went viral. He picked up a glossy wife too, somewhere along the way. These days he's running a boat agency selling floating gin palaces. You'll have to get him to show you around one. I gather his selling technique involves lots of champagne with a trip round the bay,' Sabine said.

'Haven't been on a boat since I left here.' Harriet picked up a handful of nuts from the dish Sabine had brought up with the wine. 'I had a nostalgic wander around town yesterday. Things have changed so little, I could almost believe I'd never left.'

The doorbell rang. 'That'll be dinner,' Sabine said. 'One of the posh restaurants in town does a home delivery service for special occasions. Champagne's in the fridge downstairs. Can you open it while I get dinner?'

'Right, fill me in on your life,' Sabine said as she placed a plate of French charcuterie on the table alongside a basket containing a baguette. The aroma from the garlic sausage, the mushroom pâté and mounds of black and green olives made Harriet realise how hungry she was.

'How did you survive after you left here? Where did you meet Frank?' Sabine asked as they began to eat.

'With difficulty,' Harriet said, remembering those first despairing months of being on her own with Ellie. 'I rented a small cottage in the wilds of West Wales. It was pretty bleak. I couldn't work because of Ellie so we didn't have a lot to live on. When she went to nursery school I managed to get a part-time job in a little boutique and things became a bit easier.'

'What about Oscar? Didn't he contribute?'

Harriet shook her head. 'He didn't know where we were, any more than I knew where he was. I didn't want any contact with him. It was Ellie and me against the world. Until I met Frank, who has loved and looked after us both ever since.'

'So what are you doing in town now? Is Frank with you? Do I get to meet him?'

'Not this visit. Maybe if I come down again.' Harriet paused. 'Trevor Bagshawe tracked me down and summoned me to a meeting. Amy has apparently left Ellie and me her Swannaton house. That's classified information, by the way,' she said. 'No-one else knows.'

'Apparently?'

'There's a certain clause that I have to agree to before it becomes official.' Harriet swallowed a large mouthful of her champagne. 'I'll give you three guesses what it is.'

'Amy wants you to ... to swim the Dart naked.'

Harriet giggled. 'No, Beeny, don't be daft.'

'Okay. You have to ... take up hang-gliding. No?' Sabine topped up both their glasses. 'I've really no idea.'

'One last guess,' Harriet said.

'I know. You have to give up drink. That might be hard but not impossible.'

Harriet shook her head. 'Much harder than that. I have to promise to come and live in the house for a year,' she said quietly.

'Really? That's the clause? But why is that impossible?'

Harriet looked at her wide-eyed. 'Come back after what happened? Be a laughing stock again? No thanks.'

'You weren't a laughing stock – I felt for you and other people did too. If it's any consolation, I made life as difficult as I could for the bitch before they left town too.'

'Still don't think it's a good idea to come back,' Harriet said.

'Tatty, the world has moved on. Besides, nobody cares about old scandals.'

'I do. I was the one who had to live through it. And any of our friends – like Owen and Gus – who still live in town, they'll remember.'

Sabine sighed. 'But it's so different these days. People have affairs all the time. Steal other people's husbands. It's not right, but it happens. People simply shrug and look the other way.' She was quiet for a moment before saying. 'I was tempted to do it myself once.'

Chapter Nine

Harriet

At Sabine's insistence, Harriet walked out to Amy's house the next morning.

'I'd come with you,' Sabine had said, 'but I think it's better if you go on your own for the first time. Bound to be emotional and you can indulge in private. Take tissues!'

Now, as she pushed open the driveway gate, Harriet felt the memories beginning to stir. Shrubs that hadn't been pruned for months snatched at her clothes as she walked towards the front door. Sad to see the garden so neglected when Amy had been such a keen gardener. The heavy wooden front door needed a big push to persuade it to open after Harriet had inserted and turned the key.

As she walked into the hallway, she half expected to be accosted by the smell of baking scones, a hint of beeswax on the highly polished hall-stand and Bonnie, Amy's Springer Spaniel, barking a mad welcome. Instead, silence and dusty furniture greeted her while a musty smell assailed her nostrils, a few letters and junk mail lay on the doormat.

The door to the room on the right Harriet remembered being used as a spare bedroom was ajar and Harriet pushed it open further to take a quick look inside. Bedroom furniture had been banished. Instead, a flat-screen Apple computer dominated a desk placed under the far window overlooking the side garden, a high-backed office chair pushed to one side in front of it. A stack of manila folders was on the right-hand side of the desk. The bookcase running down the length of the left wall was crammed with books, both classics and modern and several of Harriet's own favourite authors like Veronica Henry, Katie Fforde and lots of Cassandra James, one of Harriet's favourite authors.

Idly, Harriet took one she hadn't read off the shelf and thumbed slowly through it. More books were piled on the floor. Against the other wall the old fashioned roll-top desk that Harriet remembered Amy inheriting from her father was closed. Strange, Amy had never had an office in the old days.

Harriet turned and walked the few steps to the entrance of the small winter sitting room. This was much as she remembered it. Two winged armchairs, a two-seater leather Chesterfield, all facing the small open fireplace, a sheepskin rug in front. More full bookshelves, a side table or two – one with a silver tray, a decanter half full with sherry, another with whisky and three glasses. Family photos lined the mantelpiece.

Ellie in Amy's arms at her christening, dressed in the long lace dress handed down through the family. A picture of herself with a baby Ellie in her arms sitting out in the garden. Another had Ellie sleeping peacefully in her pram. A black-and-white faded one of Amy's parents. Ellie's grandparents, whom she'd never had the chance to truly bond with.

Thoughtfully, Harriet picked up one of the silver framed photos. A smiling Ellie in her bridesmaid dress for Sabine's wedding. A mere eighteen months old, she'd been so good on that day. The mantelpiece was a time warp of her and Ellie's long-ago life. Guiltily, she replaced the photo.

Amy had truly adored Ellie and the rift was in no way her fault. She hadn't been her brother's keeper. By cutting contact with her, Harriet knew she was guilty of punishing the wrong person. And now it was too late to make amends.

Smothering a sigh, Harriet moved towards the main summer sitting room. This room, with its huge sliding windows, overlooking the terrace and the mouth of the river, was light and airy. Tentatively Harriet ran her fingers over the keys of the baby grand piano positioned in the corner and in front of the side window so the pianist had an inspiring view up river. She'd always loved this room. Ellie had taken her very first steps on the ancient carpet that still covered the wooden floorboards. She'd spent so much time in this house when she and Amy had been family.

It was when she walked into the large farmhouse-style kitchen that the tears finally started and she frantically searched for a tissue. It was all still so familiar.

The large Aga cooker, the pine table where eight or ten of them would gather for one of Amy's delicious suppers and put the world to rights fuelled by a couple of bottles of wine. The dresser filled with Amy's collection of blue-and-white china. Surely any moment now, Amy herself would open the back door and come in, her gardening trug filled with vegetables, urging everyone to stay for lunch.

Taking the letter the solicitor had given her out of her pocket, Harriet pulled out one of the wheel-backed chairs and sat at the table. Had saving this to read here been a good idea? Perhaps reading it somewhere neutral would be better. Or even waiting for Frank and opening it together. No. It was her past that was involved. A time when Frank hadn't been around to protect and look after her.

Carefully she opened the envelope. Maybe it would explain things. Tell her where the money for the huge legacy had come from for instance. More importantly, explain why Amy had made the bequest.

My dearest Harriet,

Sadly we've not seen each other for many years but I've thought of you so often. You and Ellie. I hope you were able to re-build your life and eventually find happiness again. I wish you had felt able to keep in contact but do understand your reasons for severing your old life completely from the new one you were forced to face. From the day you married my brother, you became my family. In all the years, I have never thought of you as anything other than my sister-in-law.

I know Trevor Bagshawe will have explained my wishes to you and your initial response will probably be to shout NO, NO, but please think about it carefully before you decide to turn my legacy down. It is my way of making up for all the hurt you suffered at the hands of my family all those years ago. Money does not equate happiness, I am well aware, but it does provide opportunities that would otherwise be impossible. I hope it will give Ellie the chance to explore and live her life to the full.

It is not my intention to cause you more distress, but I very much long for Ellie to know her true family origins. I dreamt for years of seeing you and Ellie happy in this house again.

With much love,

Amy

Harriet's skin tingled as she read the letter. Inside her head, Amy's soft Devonshire voice was saying the words as she read them. The tears were falling freely as she finished reading and she searched in her bag for another tissue. She'd hurt Amy more than she'd ever realised with her determination to sever all contact with the family and the town. Amy had written to her about six months after the scandal broke, asking her to keep in touch, but she hadn't replied. Being genuinely fond of Amy, she'd longed to but, in the end, the need for a completely new life had won and she'd torn the letter up.

The chair scraped across the floor tiles as Harriet stood up and pushed it back. Sitting here in Amy's kitchen on her own was unnerving. All those long-ago feelings of hurt, uncertainty, guilt – oh the guilt – were flooding back.

She'd seen enough for today. She'd come back with Frank. She folded the letter back into the envelope and placed it in her bag. No information there about where the money had come from. Maybe Amy won the Lotto or something. Investments? No way of knowing. Simply that she wanted Ellie to have it.

As she walked towards the front door, her mobile rang. Ellie.

'Mum, is it all right if I come home for a bit?'

'Yes, of course. When are you coming?'

'Be with you in about an hour,' Ellie laughed. 'Sorry to spring it on you.'

'That's fine but ... have you got your key? Because neither Dad nor I are home at the moment.'

'Oh. Where are you?'

'Dad's on a business trip and I'm in Devon – having a short break.' No need to explain why. 'Ellie, is everything all right? You sound a bit hyper. I can come home this evening if you need me.'

'Everything is fine. Just got an unexpected holiday. Enjoy your break. I'll see you when you get back. Love you.'

'Love you too,' Harriet said as the call ended. Something had happened in Ellie's life, she was sure. She was too determinedly cheerful. What did 'coming home for a bit' mean in reality?

The river was sparkling in the noon-day sun as Harriet walked back into town deep in thought. She'd promised to meet Sabine at the kiosk for a picnic lunch.

Sabine had a small crowd round her as Harriet approached, so she hung back watching the passenger ferry and looking at the river scene. Far more boats and moorings in the river than she remembered.

Once Sabine had finished dealing with the holidaymakers, she opened a couple of the director's chairs and placed them on the embankment pavement.

'How did it go up at the house? Pasty and wine okay?' she asked. Without waiting for an answer to her second question, she handed Harriet a plastic cup of red wine. 'Pasties will be here soon.'

'It was weird. After all these years it was as if I'd never been away,' Harriet said. 'I kept expecting Amy to appear and tell me off for not telling her I was popping in and why hadn't I brought Ellie.' She took a sip of the wine. 'I can't tell you how guilty I feel over Amy. I wish I could say sorry to her. Make up for the lost years.'

'Doing what she wants and living in the house could be one way,' Sabine said.

'But she won't know, will she?' Harriet sighed. 'It's too late.'

Their pasties were delivered just then by a young lad on an old-fashioned bicycle with a large wicker basket fixed to the front. For several minutes both women ate contentedly.

'Gosh these are good,' Harriet said. 'Haven't had a pasty in years.' She glanced at Sabine, who'd muttered an oath.

'Just seen Owen coming this way. Didn't think when I suggested lunch here that certain other people would be around. Sorry.'

Harriet shrugged. 'Not to worry.' Managing two days incognito in her home town had to be some sort of record anyway.

'Hi, Owen,' Sabine said. 'Guess who's turned up?'

'Harriet, nice to see you. I'd heard you were back and wondered if we'd meet.'

Harriet glanced at Sabine, who held up her hands. 'I swear I didn't tell him. Who did?' she said glaring at Owen.

'Can't remember,' Owen said, shrugging. 'Staying long?'

Harriet shook her head. 'Just a few days.'

'Sabine filling you in with all the news?'

'Hear you've done really well with the business,' Harriet said.

'She tell you I'm off at the end of the season for a bit of travelling? Try to persuade her to come with me, will you? Right. I'm off to have lunch with the mayor – want to bend his ear about this kiosk. I'll be back for the 2.30 trip. Don't forget to sign the Save the Kiosk petition, Harriet.'

As he left them, Harriet looked at Sabine, 'Travelling with Owen?'

Sabine shrugged. 'Told him I'll think about it, that's all, but it's not going to happen.'

'Could be fun.'

'Mmm,' Sabine said. 'More wine?'

'No thanks. Have to drive to Totnes later to meet Frank,' Harriet said. 'Oh, Beeny what am I going to do?'

'Selfishly, I want you to come back! It all happened so long ago I can't see it affecting your life now. People won't even realise you're a true local unless you tell them. They'll think you're another incomer. And old friends will just accept that you're back.'

Harriet looked at Sabine. 'You make it sound so easy.'

'Accept the legacy, Tatty. Worry about it afterwards. Ten to one, there won't be half the problems you imagine happening.'

'Even if that proves to be true – what about Ellie's reaction? I'm terrified she'll hate me for my past mistakes.'

Harriet scrunched up the plastic cup and threw it in a nearby waste bin. 'I'd better go and let you get on with selling tickets.'

Impulsively she hugged Sabine. 'Oh it's so good to be back together. Why did we ever lose touch?'

'Because you did a runner, you daft bitch,' Sabine said.

Harriet laughed. Beeny never had been one to hold back.

Four hours later, Harriet, sitting in the car at Totnes railway station waiting for Frank, mentally went over the pros and cons regarding Amy's legacy.

Accepting and going back to live in the town – could she really do it? The condition of living in the house for a year wasn't that long, really. If it didn't work out at the end of the twelve months, she could return home and use the house simply as a holiday home. Or even rent it out. The last few days had shown her that she still had friends in the town and the warm fuzzy feeling she'd always got driving down the hill towards the Higher Ferry whenever she'd been away for some reason, had hit her hard the day she'd arrived. Deep down, she knew she wanted to live back in the town.

Ellie's reaction was the real worry. There was so much she didn't know about the past. Would it all have to come out when she was told about the legacy? The scandal itself might have happened a long time ago and, like Beeny said, people were more forgiving because it was so commonplace these days, but how would Ellie react to her mother's secret. She wouldn't have to tell Ellie anything about the past if she turned the inheritance down, but how could she live with herself if she did that? Besides, she and Frank had always said they would tell Ellie the truth about the past when the time was right. Now Amy's legacy had catapulted into their lives, the moment couldn't be denied any longer. Whatever the consequences.

And Frank? How would all this affect their relationship? Would he be prepared to move with her to the town she'd vowed never to return to? Could his work commitments even make it impossible for him to live in Devon? No, that wasn't a reason for not returning. These days the Internet made it possible to live and work anywhere.

Harriet reached into her bag and took out Amy's letter and turned it over and over. She didn't need to read it again. She'd read it so many times now she could have recited the contents word for word if she'd been asked. Intriguing that Amy had anticipated her saying no to the legacy. There were so many reasons to turn it down – and just the one for accepting – whatever the problems it brought her, Harriet, there was no denying it was Ellie's birth right. How could she possibly deny her?

Getting out of the car as the London express pulled into the station, Harriet sighed. She and Frank would discuss it but, in truth, there was only one decision they could make …

Chapter Ten

Ellie

Parking in her parents' driveway, Ellie sat for a few moments physically unable to summon up the energy to actually get out of the car. Gripping the steering wheel, she banged her head against it in despair. God what a twenty-four hours. Job and home gone simultaneously.

In one way she was relieved her parents were away and she didn't have to face them, but on the other hand she longed for a hug from her dad and a gruff 'It'll sort itself, pet', his answer to everything that had upset her throughout life. Mum would give her a quick cuddle and make her a hot chocolate before sitting down, prepared to listen to all the ins and outs of what had gone wrong this time.

She was stiff when she finally got out of the car and went into the house. She'd unpack the car later. Not that there was a lot of stuff. Mainly clothes and a few personal items that were lying about. She'd literally flown around the flat pushing things into her large rucksack, knowing deep down she was unlikely to see anything she'd missed ever again. She sighed deeply. Right now, she needed a coffee.

Once in the kitchen, she switched the machine on and heaped coffee into the filter. Waiting for the water to drip through, she wandered upstairs to her old room. Now technically the guest room, it lacked the funky wallpaper and posters she'd pinned up everywhere in her teenage years before leaving home. For the past five years the walls had been covered in a bland cream paper with nondescript twirls on it. The old-fashioned kidney-shaped dressing table still stood in front of the window, the ruched material concealing its drawers and central shelf the same toile de jouy pattern that hung at the window. Rod had been scathing: 'God, this room belongs in the last century.' He'd been dismissive of everything else in the house too. Oh, not to Harriet and Frank. To them he was charm itself. It was just to her in private that he poked fun. When she'd protested he was being unkind, he'd just looked at her and shrugged.

Ellie went back downstairs. After pouring her coffee and helping herself to a couple of biscuits from the tin, she went into the sitting room and flopped onto the settee. How naive she'd been to waste nine months of her life with him, thinking they were good together. That he might actually love her. She should have known when he didn't introduce her to his parents for months.

'Plenty of time for that,' he kept saying, as if he didn't want to introduce her to them. When he had taken her home, the visit hadn't been a success. The family had treated her like a difficult guest for the whole visit.

Rod had met Frank and Harriet early on in their relationship – and that hadn't been a great success either. Mum hadn't taken to him at all, and as for Frank, he'd been a typical growly dad thinking nobody was good enough for his girl. Thinking back, from the time she'd moved into the flat, their relationship had changed. Rod always busy at work, their social life non-existent except for the occasional cinema visit and then it was always his choice. How had she failed to notice just how self-centred Rod was? How selfish. Clearly she'd been useful to pay the rent. She hadn't just been naive – she'd been plain stupid.

At nearly thirty years old, you'd have thought she'd have known better. She'd been so desperate for a relationship, the chance to finally settle down and maybe start a family, she'd overlooked so much. Was she destined never to find her soulmate? Never to have a lasting loving relationship? Her track record wasn't good in that department, that was for sure. Mum had once told her she was too trusting. Well, not any more. This was the last time she was going to jump into any relationship without first analysing every single aspect of the man in question.

Draining the last of her coffee, Ellie got to her feet and stretched. Time to get her stuff out of the car. Tomorrow she'd start the dual business of job and flat hunting. By the time Mum and Dad came home, she'd be organised and on her way to sorting her life out.

Chapter Eleven

Sabine

May Bank Holiday Monday found Sabine huddled in the kiosk with the heater on and just the top half of the stable door hitched open. Thankfully without any wind behind it, the rain wasn't blowing into the kiosk. The town was always crowded over the Bank Holiday whatever the weather, and Sabine was busy selling tickets for the 11 o'clock trip up river.

Holidaymakers, desperate to find something to do out of the rain, had decided a trip on the Queen of the River, with its below deck saloon and bar, was ideal. It wasn't as if the river was rough. No wind making the water choppy, just rain, rain, rain. What better way to pass the last day of the long weekend than gliding up river with a glass of wine in hand. Lunch in Totnes and then back down to Dartmouth before beginning the long trek back home courtesy of the A38 and the M5. Personally, Sabine would have been happy if she could just have stayed at home in this weather and curled up with a good book.

By half past ten the boat was fully booked and Sabine was turning people away. She was just thinking about putting the kettle on for a coffee when Johnnie appeared, waving a bag of warm doughnuts at her.

'Coffee here or at the cottage?'

'Your place,' Sabine said. 'Much cosier today. Give me twenty minutes to see everybody on board and I'll be with you. Don't eat all the doughnuts before I get there.'

Sabine was locking the kiosk as Queen of the River began to move away from the landing stage when BB walked past.

'Morning. Care to join me for a drink?'

'Sorry. My brother is expecting me for coffee and doughnuts at his place.' Sabine hesitated. 'Want to come? You can talk boats.'

'Sure would.'

As they walked through town, Sabine said, 'So whereabouts in American are you from?'

'Small town on the coast of South Carolina,' BB answered. 'Ever been to America?'

Sabine shook her head. 'No. Nearly went once when I was younger but sadly life got in the way. Might put a visit to the USA on my bucket list.'

'Well, if you ever make it over to South Carolina you make sure to find me and the family. You'd be made right welcome.'

'Thank you, BB. Right, Johnnie's cottage is down this lane.' She led the way up to a navy-blue door and turned the handle.

'Johnnie, I've brought a friend. Would like to talk to you about boats, I think.'

Once the introductions were made, and BB was admiring the framed pictures of various boats Johnnie had hanging everywhere, Sabine made the coffee and took it through into the sitting room.

Talk naturally turned to boats and sailing and BB started to tell Johnnie the kind of thing he was hoping to find. Sipping her coffee, Sabine tuned out from the conversation.

Telling BB she'd put a visit to the US on her bucket list had reminded her about Owen and his plans. Was the US on his itinerary to visit? She'd have to ask him. Going with someone would be fun. She'd never liked the idea of travelling alone. Wonder where else was he planning to go? She'd always fancied seeing Italy, Mexico too. If she agreed to go with Owen they could plan a list of destinations between them. India could be fascinating too. He'd said 'no strings'. They could be geriatric back-packers together – couch-surfing their way around the world for six months. She smiled at the thought. Owen was always good company.

She was jerked out of her daydream when BB stood up.

'Thanks for the coffee. I'd best get going. Thought I'd head over to Kingswear marina today, see if they've got anything interesting on their books.'

'See you around,' Sabine said and Johnnie politely got up to see him out.

'Nice bloke,' Johnnie said as the front door slammed behind BB.

'You know he's looking for somewhere to live for summer?' Sabine said. 'Ever thought of taking a lodger? Be company for you. Wouldn't have to worry about the place when you were away.'

'God, no,' Johnnie said. 'I need my own space. Can't bear the idea of a stranger – however nice he is – being here.' He hesitated. 'Anyway, I'm thinking about selling this place.'

Sabine looked at him, surprised.

'It's over three years since Annie died. You sold up and moved much quicker after Dave. Kick-started a new life for you and Peter. Think it's about time I did the same.'

'I know you and Annie loved this place, but you'll always have the memories,' Sabine said gently. 'Wherever you live.'

'Might sell the boat too and use all the money to buy a bigger one and live on board.'

'Good idea,' Sabine said. At last Johnnie was beginning to think about his future.

'Owen told you about his plans for a six-month sabbatical?'

Johnnie shook his head. 'No. When's he planning to go? And where?'

'End of the season. Not sure which countries exactly – Europe obviously.' Sabine paused before adding, 'He's asked me to go with him.'

'You going?'

'Told him I'd think about it. But if I go, I'd like to see more than just Europe. Mexico, India and Iceland. Places like that appeal. Just a bit worried about what people might think. Him and me going off together, because it wouldn't be like that.'

'Might be before you come back,' Johnnie teased. 'India. The Taj Mahal. We all know how romantic that place is.' Sabine poked her tongue out at him.

Johnnie hesitated before adding, 'He's a good bloke. Been in love with you for years.'

'I know,' Sabine said. 'I kind of love him too but ...' She shrugged and decided to change the subject. 'See you've got a letter from Martha,' she said pointing at the letter lying on the coffee table. 'Any interesting news?'

'Bit strange really. Here, read it.' Johnnie picked it up and handed it to her. 'Tell me what you think.'

Sabine quickly scanned the letter before looking up at him. 'Not like Martha, is it? Maybe ring her?'

'Done that. All she would say is that she needs to talk to me in person and the sooner the better.'

'It's probably just French bureaucracy getting its knickers in a twist over something and she needs some advice,' Sabine said.

Johnny nodded. 'I'll go over soon for a quick visit between deliveries. Help her sort whatever it is.'

'Make sure you're back for my exhibition. I need you here for support,' Sabine said.

Chapter Twelve

BB

BB walked out of the letting agency's office depressed. He'd been so confident he'd be able to find somewhere other than the hotel to live for summer, but as the weeks went by it seemed a fruitless search. All the agency could offer him was a week here and there in various holiday lets. The idea of having to move house several times during the summer didn't appeal.

'The problem,' the girl in the office explained, 'is that owners already have bookings for most of the summer. Nobody in town on our books has anything available for a long let. Maybe if you'd consider Stoke Fleming or Strete, I'd be able to find you something.'

He'd shaken his head at her suggestion. 'I really want to stay in town – besides, I don't have any transport.'

Walking through town ten minutes later on his way back to the hotel, he decided to let things ride for a bit. No choice really. Besides, it wasn't that he couldn't afford to stay at the hotel, it was just he wanted somewhere he could relax and not have to worry about sticking to a schedule for breakfast and vacating the room for the maid. Admittedly it was nice having the bed-making and cleaning etc. done every day. Perhaps staying put and having all the domestic bits of life taken care of was the sensible thing to do. Allow him to concentrate on investigating the family tree and finding a boat.

He knew from the papers at home that had started him on this quest to find 'The English Connection' as Jessica had dubbed it, their Grandma Mary had been Mary Seale, the only daughter of William and Amelia Seale, before she ran away with the love of her life, Grandpa Millman, and been disowned by her English family.

A quick glance in the phone book at the hotel had told him there were no families of either name left in the town, so no convenient door to knock on hoping for quick leads. He ordered a beer, took it over to a table in the corner and began to trawl through the property pages of the day's paper again on the off chance he'd missed something on his first read. What he'd really love to find would be somewhere like Johnnie's ancient cottage. He been tempted to ask if he had a spare room. So full of atmosphere, he could only wonder at the stories it could tell. A house like that would be amazing.

Five minutes later, he folded the paper up in frustration. Nothing. He glanced at his watch. A couple of hours to kill before his appointment with the yacht broker down at the marina. Apparently they were keen for him to see a fifty-foot wooden ketch that had just been put up for sale over in Brixham.

Before then he had time to wander along the quay and take another look at Bayards Cove. It was a place that fascinated him. Made him wish his ancestors had gone over with the Pilgrims back in the seventeenth century rather than running away to marry a GI three centuries later. He also needed to visit the library and spend some time there looking up the history of the town with particular regard to the Holdsworths and the Seales, whom he'd already discovered had run the town a couple of centuries ago.

Then this evening he'd return to his room and spend the evening reading and doing some more research on the Internet. He didn't want Jessie telling him he wasn't doing enough to find their 'English Connection'.

HIGH SEASON

Chapter Thirteen

Johnnie

Johnnie stood patiently in line at the cash desk while the woman being served carefully placed her shopping in her wheelie bag before handing the cashier her cheque book. He could sense the impatience of the couple in front of him before they tutted loudly but it didn't bother him.

'They should try queuing in a French supermarket,' a voice behind him said softly. 'This is so quick compared. Takes hours sometimes over there to do a weekly shop.'

He turned and saw the woman who'd helped him secure Annie on the grid the other week. Probably not a holidaymaker then.

'Hello. You're right about French supermarkets – takes forever to do a quick shop.'

'We both like good French wine though,' she said, indicating the same bottle in their respective baskets.

'You know about wine?'

'Just a bit.'

Johnnie started to place his stuff on the conveyor belt, carefully laying down the wine to avoid it toppling over when the belt jerked forward.

'Morning, Johnnie,' the female cashier said, flashing his items through. 'Everything okay?'

'Fine,' he answered, handing over some notes. He pocketed his change, picked his shopping up, smiled at the two women and left. Two minutes later, he was loitering outside, wishing the woman would hurry up and appear.

The woman glanced at him and smiled when he fell into step alongside her.

'As one sailor to another – can I buy you a coffee?' he said. 'The Royal is the nearest place if that's all right with you?'

'Thank you, Johnnie, that would be lovely.'

'How do you know my name? Ah …' Comprehension dawned. 'Susie on the cash desk. That's the trouble with being a local – so you're …?'

'Rachel.'

'Thought you might be a holidaymaker the other day,' Johnnie said.

She shook her head. 'No. I live in town now.'

The Harbour Bar was busy as they entered, with both locals and holidaymakers enjoying a mid-morning coffee. One or two of the locals raised their hands in greeting to Johnnie as he went to order their coffees. He saw BB tucked away in a quiet corner, intently studying the local newspaper, oblivious to anyone around him.

Sitting with another women in a place where he and Annie had often had coffee felt strange. Of course he'd been in here often enough in the past year or two with Sabine and friends, but it had been a long time since he'd actually invited a woman to have coffee with him. He stirred his coffee thoughtfully, wondering what to say. BB, on his way out, walked over.

'Hi, Johnnie, how you doing?' BB said.

Johnnie stood up and quickly introduced Rachel before saying, 'Found anywhere to live yet?'

BB shook his head. 'Been through the papers again today. No luck. Wouldn't be a problem if I wanted to stay the other side of the river for the summer, but here it's proving impossible to find anything – even a room rather than an apartment.'

'I've a spare room,' Rachel said quietly. 'It has an en-suite bathroom, but you'd have to share the kitchen and the sitting room with me.'

Both BB and Johnnie looked at her.

'Really?' BB said. 'I have a feeling you're about to turn into my Fairy Godmother.'

Rachel laughed. 'You haven't seen the room yet and for all you know I might be the stuff nightmares are made of. The landlady from hell.'

'I doubt that. When can I come and see the room?' BB said.

'How about coming for a drink this evening? About 7.30? Give me time to sort things. I haven't been in the house long and I've been using that room as a general dumping ground.'

'Great. Where are you?'

'Clarence Hill. You know it?'

As BB nodded and Rachel told him the number, Johnnie found himself thinking, that's one of the older houses not far from me.

'See you this evening then.' And BB was gone.

'Well that was unexpected,' Rachel said, drinking her coffee. 'Thanks for suggesting coming here and introducing me to BB.'

'He's just a new acquaintance my sister introduced me to,' Johnnie said awkwardly. 'I don't really know anything about him – he could be a serial killer or anything. Although he seems nice enough,' he added quickly.

Rachel smiled. 'Oh, Johnnie, I'm sure he's not going to murder me in my bed. If he does, I'll come back and haunt you for introducing us. He's just an ordinary guy looking for somewhere to stay. Reminds me of my son, although I think he's a bit older.'

She pushed her empty coffee cup and saucer away. 'I don't know you either – but I'm fairly certain you're okay.' She laughed at the expression on his face.

'You have a son?' Johnnie said.

Rachel nodded. 'Yes, he lives in France with his family. He's a great sailor too,' she added. 'He'd love your boat – *Annie*, isn't she called? It's been years since I've set foot on a wooden boat. They tended to be all fibreglass where we lived.' She glanced at Johnnie, hesitating, totally unsure whether she should say what she was about to.

'If you ever need a crew, remember me, won't you?'

'Usually sail singlehanded,' Johnnie said, not mentioning that he preferred it that way since Annie had died. Couldn't imagine anyone taking her place on the boat. 'The boat's named after my late wife.'

But then, to his own surprise, he heard himself adding, 'Actually, I've got to go across to France sometime soon. Not keen on doing the channel single-handed, so I usually get one of the pros from the agency I work for to come with me, but if you'd be interested?'

'You serious?' Rachel said. When he nodded she said, 'I'd love to. I don't know the north coast of France at all. Just give me twenty-four hours notice and I'll be there, Cap'n.' She gave him a salute before holding out her hand for him to shake.

'Right, I'd better get going. Prepare things for my prospective lodger. Thanks for the coffee.'

Johnnie watched her walk out of the restaurant wondering why on earth he hadn't kept his mouth shut. As he'd shaken her hand, he'd clocked the wedding ring. Hell, he hadn't even thought to ask if there was a husband on the scene when she mentioned her son. He could only pray there wasn't – or at least not one who would object to his wife sailing away with another man for a few days. But surely she'd have mentioned a husband if she had one? Especially when she offered BB a room. Oh well, he'd find out on his next trip to France. He'd find out whether she was a real sailor then too.

Rachel might profess to love sailing and tie a good knot, but would she be any good as crew? So long as she could steer a course and winch a sail or two up, everything should be fine. Shouldn't it?

Chapter Fourteen

Rachel

Walking home, Rachel wondered about Johnnie's wife. How had she died? How long ago? Had she been a local girl? He definitely didn't want to talk about her, that was for sure. He'd left the sentence about the boat's name hanging in the air without any other explanation.

Rachel stroked her wedding ring with her thumb, making it slide around her finger. She'd registered Johnnie looking at her wedding ring. A year since her world had fallen apart, but still she couldn't bring herself to take the ring off. Johnnie hadn't asked about her husband but then, she hadn't volunteered the information either.

Johnnie had probably assumed she was divorced as most people did before she told them she was a widow. Maybe he didn't have any intention of asking her to crew for him. Maybe he was just being polite to her face and would forget the conversation. He hadn't asked about any commitments that might stop her going to France with him.

Not that there were any these days. She was as free as a bird. No-one to worry about, which was one of the reasons she hoped BB would like the room. There would have to be ground rules, of course, but it would be good to have somebody else in the cottage, somebody to maybe share a glass or two of wine out on the terrace of an evening. Having someone to house-sit the cottage if she did crew for Johnnie on this trip to France would be a welcome bonus.

The spare room wasn't as bad as she'd feared. Just a couple of boxes she hadn't unpacked yet – she wasn't even sure what was in them if she was honest. They could go in the basement for now. Open the window, a quick vacuum and dust, make the bed, clean the en suite, find some towels and another bath mat and she was done. Quite like old times when the villa had been full of friends and she'd won the accolade of 'Hostess with the Mostest'.

Would it suit BB though? Maybe he was looking for something more upmarket, something more along the lines of his room at The Royal. Oh well, if he didn't like it at least she'd sorted the spare room.

BB, when he arrived promptly at 7.30, was carrying a bunch of flowers which he handed to her with a smile.

'Thank you. I'll just put them in water,' Rachel said. 'Then I'll show you the room.'

Leading the way upstairs, she said, 'I have to warn you it's not a very big room.'

'It's perfect,' BB said, taking it in with a glance. 'It's got everything I need. Can I move in tomorrow?'

Rachel laughed. 'We haven't discussed rent yet. Or how long you'd like to stay. And there will be a few ground rules.' She looked at him anxiously. 'You're not a smoker, are you? If you are, then I'm afraid it's not on anyway.'

'No, not a smoker and I have to return to the States in September, so from now until then?'

'Let's go and have a glass of wine and discuss the terms and conditions then,' Rachel said.

Sitting on her small terrace sharing a bottle of rosé, Rachel laid down the ground rules as she thought of them.

'I'll give you a key so you'll be free to come and go as you like. I'm happy to provide toast and coffee for breakfast but any other food you want, you'll have to buy. I'll clear a shelf in the fridge for you. I have to warn you, I can't stand a messy kitchen so make sure you clear up after yourself.'

'I'm not a bad cook but I'll probably eat out most days,' BB said. 'Talking of food. If you haven't eaten, will you join me for dinner tonight? Celebrate our deal?'

'Thank you,' Rachel said. 'You're certainly starting off on the right foot. First flowers and now dinner. I'll just get a cardigan.'

BB was looking at a photo of Rachel and a younger man in a silver frame on the mantelpiece of the sitting room when she came back downstairs.

'My son,' Rachel said. 'Taken a couple of years ago. You may get to meet Hugo. He and his wife are hoping to come for a visit later in the year.'

Chapter Fifteen

Ellie

Ellie had placed her laptop on the table in front of the window in her old bedroom and was rapidly turning the space around it into her office. So far she'd refrained from sending her CV out to prospective employers, deciding instead to freelance for a bit. See if she could earn enough money to survive that way.

Thanks to Estelle, she'd been commissioned to write three features with more promised in the next few weeks. She'd also been busy pitching some story ideas to a couple of magazines where she had her own contacts, quickly realising freelancing was a numbers game – the more ideas you pitched, the more the chance of being commissioned.

She'd not yet started the hunt for a new flat either, mainly because both Mum and Dad, together and separately, had urged her to stay for as long as she liked – and had refused to take any rent, which was a big bonus until her finances were in better shape. Her redundancy money was already gathering a little bit of interest in the bank and there was still money in her current account – thanks again to Mum and Dad who were also feeding her. They'd insisted she accepted the status quo while she got back on her feet.

It was funny living back home again though. Dad was away on business a couple of days a week and Mum seemed to be living in a world of her own at the moment. To say she was preoccupied was putting it mildly. Once or twice Ellie had caught her looking at her with a funny expression on her face. When she'd asked, 'What?' her mother had shaken her head, smiled at her and said, 'Sorry, love. I was miles away.'

At least both parents had stopped tiptoeing around the subject of Rod. Her dad had been forthright in his dismissal of him. 'Never took to him if I'm honest, love. You deserve someone much, much nicer.' And he'd patted her gently on the back as he hugged her.

Mum, when Ellie had tearfully muttered she was worried about never meeting 'the one' and never having children, had hugged her tightly and said, 'You will. The right one always comes along in the end.'

Ellie had sniffed and prayed that she was right. It was three months now since Rod had cast her adrift and moved to Manchester with her replacement. Three months in which she'd been determined to get her life back on the track she wanted – never to put it on hold again for anyone. She still had the occasional teary moments, usually in bed around midnight when unsolvable problems went round and round in her head.

Thankfully, there had been fewer nightmares and midnight crises lately. But she had to face facts. She was thirty in September. The clock was ticking. She'd always expected to be married by now. All her old friends – except for Tamsyn who from sixth-form days had always vowed she'd never tie herself down to one man – were married and most had one if not more children. Although on the downside, there was poor Liz currently facing single motherhood after her sleaze of a husband had gone off with their Spanish au pair. At least she didn't have to cope with that.

Switching on her laptop, Ellie picked up a pile of papers on her desk and began to flick through them as she waited for it to boot up. She'd been amazed to discover these tattered pages of a novel she'd started about ten years ago at the back of her wardrobe yesterday – she'd thought she'd thrown all her old notebooks and jottings away when she'd left home.

Now, giving the manuscript a quick read through prior to finally throwing it away, she found herself intrigued by the words she'd written so long ago. She remembered how inspired she'd been when the idea for the novel had first occurred to her.

Thoughtfully she sat back. Ever since she could hold a crayon, she'd drawn and written stories, as a teenager she'd dreamt of being a bestselling novelist. Everybody knew novelists struggled unless they hit the big time bigger than big. Being a writer meant a life on the breadline with no job security, no regular wage, no pension in the dim and distant future. Something both Harriet and Frank had urged her to think about when choosing a career.

Becoming a journalist had seemed the sensible option for a career involving writing. For the last eight years she'd enjoyed writing up news and features – she'd even won a prestigious 'Young Journalist of the Year' award in the early days soon after she'd left journalism school.

Redundancy had changed things though. Proved that there was no such thing as job security these days. So why not take the opportunity and become a novelist – or at least give it a try. To be truthful, she hadn't thought about writing fiction for years but now the idea had popped into her brain, it refused to go away.

If she treated the freelance writing of articles as her 'proper' 9–5 job, she'd have money coming in and she could write her fiction in the evenings. Maybe even go on a Creative Writing course to get her into the mind-set of writing fiction.

Resolutely Ellie pulled her laptop towards her, opened a new file and titled it 'Novel'. She'd make a start by editing and typing in the twenty thousand words or so she'd written all those years ago and seeing if there was potential there. If not, she'd think of another idea.

Chapter Sixteen

Harriet

Harriet poured herself a welcome G&T before wandering into the sitting room and looking around. God she was tired and stiff after two days of cleaning, doing mountains of washing and ironing and re-organising the house, but it looked so much better. More like it had looked in Amy's day. Wooden surfaces were polished, curtains freshly washed and ironed hung at all the gleaming windows downstairs – the upstairs curtains would have to wait until her next visit.

She'd bravely pressed the ignition button for the gas-fired Aga Thursday evening when she'd arrived, praying it would work. Thankfully it had and the kitchen was now nice and toasty with the warmth drifting through to the rest of the house. Fanciful she knew, but she'd swear she could sense Amy's pleased presence all around her.

The small sitting room was cheerful, warmed by a log fire with wood she'd unearthed in the garden shed. Two silver candleholders stood alone on the mantelpiece, the family photos banished to a drawer in the study until she showed them to Ellie. The only room she hadn't touched downstairs was Amy's study.

She'd only been in there once this visit and that was to pick up a book for reading in bed. A quick look in the roll-top desk had convinced her it was full of really private stuff – letters and papers Amy wouldn't have wanted a stranger rifling through. Not that she was a stranger, of course, but even so.

Hidden in the study cupboard too were the few personal items she'd brought down with her – photos, books, cushions and her favourite table lamp. She'd debated about displaying them in the small sitting room but decided against it.

As far as Ellie was concerned, until they'd had 'The Talk', this was just a house they were renting for a short family break in a few weeks time. Once Ellie had been told the truth, then the photos and personal things could be placed in their new positions. She'd sighed and locked the door before hanging the key on a hook in the kitchen. Clearing the study would be her first job once she'd moved in permanently, she promised herself. Maybe Ellie could be persuaded to help.

Harriet sipped her drink, thinking about how she'd lied to Ellie – again – about this weekend. As far as Ellie was concerned, she was visiting an old friend, which was sort of true, just not the one Ellie thought she was with.

Ellie had been upbeat before she left. How determined she was to sort her life out before her big birthday in September. Talking about writing a novel. Would the news the house they were staying in – and the large personal legacy Aunt Amy had left her – would eventually be hers help or hinder in that respect? Surely help? It was the story behind the legacy that could prove to be a sticking point.

Finishing her drink, Harriet moved back into the kitchen and placed her glass in the dishwasher. Time to get ready to party.

She'd stopped by the kiosk two mornings ago after her visit to the supermarket for cleaning stuff and Beeny, thrilled to see her back, had said, 'We have to have a party to celebrate. Two ticks, my life is ruled by the tides.' She turned to look at the tide table. 'Right, eight o'clock Saturday evening, my place. I'll round up a few of the old gang and we'll have a big catch-up, get all the gossip out of the way and then you can settle down to enjoy being back.'

Harriet had tried to protest, but Sabine wasn't listening. Harriet knew Sabine was right really. Get the past thirty years out into the open, acknowledge they'd happened and then move on.

'Want me to bring anything – other than the requisite bottle of course?' she asked.

'No, don't worry. I'll just throw some pizzas in the oven. I can always send Peter out for fish and chips if we need more food.'

A quick shower, fresh jeans, knee-high boots, a pink shirt, scarf knotted around her neck and Harriet was as ready as she could be with the limited amount of clothes she'd brought with her on this trip. Grabbing her waterproof coat from the hall-stand and a torch from the table, she slammed the front door behind her and set off for Beeny's.

She was the first to arrive and helped Beeny with the final preparations, which consisted mainly of opening the wine and placing half a dozen pizzas on trays ready for the oven.

'Didn't expect so many of the old gang to still be living in town,' Harriet said. 'There's enough here to feed at least thirty people.'

'That's about right if everyone comes,' Sabine said, concentrating on pulling a particularly difficult cork out of a bottle of red wine.

Harriet looked at her, surprised. 'There was never that many in the old days.'

'A few are bringing their partners and I've also invited some of my friends. Incomers, mainly, who I thought you might like to meet. Get your social circle going for when you move down.'

Harriet sighed. 'As long as I don't have to explain why I left.'

Sabine shook her head. 'No of course not. I'll gloss over that when I introduce you. So, when are you moving in permanently?'

'Eighteenth of the month the house will become my official address for purposes of Amy's will. Solicitor has promised it will all be sorted by then,' Harriet said. 'I'm looking forward to being here for the summer now. Only drawback is it will be July before Frank can join me. It'll be a case of seeing each other at weekends for a couple of months.'

'And Ellie? Do you think she'll come down here to live?'

Harriet shrugged. 'No idea but I'm praying she will. If she gets a new job it could be anywhere – London, Bristol etc., etc. She's freelancing for a bit so she could do that from anywhere. She may of course elect to stay in Cirencester.' She glanced at Sabine. 'It also depends on how she reacts to the news. I haven't told her about the house or the legacy yet.'

'What? But you've had weeks.'

'I know, I know. I thought I'd let Trevor Bagshawe get all the legal things sorted. A few more weeks isn't going to make any difference. Besides, she's been upset over Rod and losing her job.'

'I'd say the legacy would take her mind off things nicely,' Sabine said. 'Help her decide what to do.'

'It's the questions she's going to ask about Amy and … things. She's going to want to know all the sordid details.'

Sabine shrugged. 'The world's a lot more sordid these days. Ellie is of a generation that takes these things in their stride. Chances are, she'll not see it the same way as you.'

'Frank and I are going to talk to her together soon. I'm planning a family holiday here,' Harriet said quietly. Frank had already threatened to tell Ellie the truth without her if she didn't stop putting it off.

The doorbell rang before she could say any more and Sabine went to let the first of her friends in.

Harriet sighed. Frank had repeatedly told her she was being a coward, but just the thought of telling Ellie about the past made her feel ill. Which was stupid. What woman her age didn't have a secret in their past they would rather not discuss?

'Tatty, look who's arrived,' Sabine called. 'And he's brought champagne.'

Going through into the sitting room, Harriet recognised Gus instantly. He was an older, smoother version of the man she'd last seen thirty years ago and yet there was something about the scruffy teenage boy she'd worshipped from afar still clinging to him despite the designer label clothes.

'Still as gorgeous as ever,' Gus said, kissing her on both cheeks. 'You haven't changed a bit.'

'If only that were true,' Harriet laughed. 'Thank you anyway.'

'Beeny says you're moving back?'

Harriet nodded. 'Aunt Amy's old house. I hear you're selling posh boats these days.'

'Yeah. You in the market for one? No? Shame.' This as Harriet shook her head. 'Come for a look around anyway. I guess Ellie is all grown up these days?' he added. 'Is she here?'

Harriet shook her head. 'No. We don't actually move in until the middle of next month.' She turned as someone put their arm around her.

'Harriet, how lovely to finally catch up with you.'

'Johnnie. I thought you were away on a delivery? Beeny said you probably wouldn't make it tonight.'

'Couldn't miss the welcome back party,' Johnnie said. 'I see most of the old gang are here.'

'Plus a few people I don't actually recognise or even know,' Harriet said.

Johnnie looked around. 'Want me to introduce you to anyone?'

Harriet shook her head. 'Maybe later. Right now I'll go and see if Beeny wants a hand with the pizzas. I'll catch up with you two later.'

In the kitchen Sabine was busy cutting up pizzas while a younger man heaped the slices onto serving plates.

'Tatty, this is BB. He's in town for the summer. BB, this is my oldest and best friend and the reason for the party.'

'Hi, great to meet you, Tatty. Is that a real old English name?'

Harriet laughed. 'No. My real name is Harriet. Tatty is just a nickname Beeny landed me with at school many years ago.'

'Right, let's go feed the hordes,' Sabine said.

The next couple of hours passed quickly in a nostalgic haze as old friends greeted Harriet and they exchanged memories of their long-ago shared past. Some of the memories she remembered more clearly than others but it all felt good. Many 'Expect it feels funny being back?' type questions were asked along with 'You must come for dinner when you're settled in' invitations being issued.

It did feel kind of strange in a weird way though – technically these were all old friends but, in reality, they didn't know each other at all. For the last thirty years their lives had diverged so much, was it really possible for them to turn the clock back and pick up where they'd left off?

Right now she was a returning novelty. Harriet crossed her fingers. With luck she'd be just a nine-day wonder who would soon simply fade into the background as summer rolled on.

It was midnight before the party finally began to wind down. As people started to drift away, Johnnie turned to Harriet.

'Like me to walk you out to Swannaton? Bit lonely out that way.'

Before Harriet could answer, Sabine interrupted. 'She's staying the night. Bed's already made up.'

'I am?' Harriet said.

Sabine nodded. 'No reason not to. We can have a good old natter about everyone now they've gone. Besides, you can help me clear up.'

Harriet laughed. 'Put like that, how can I refuse?'

Half an hour later, both women were up in the studio with a last plate of cold pizza and a half-full bottle of champagne, Sabine having declared the rest of the clearing up could wait until the morning.

'Thanks for tonight,' Harriet said. 'It was great to see the old gang. At one stage I felt as if I'd never been away, although a couple of people did make me feel like a newbie to town.'

'You just wait until you're back permanently,' Sabine said. 'You'll soon be roped in to join every club you can think of. Is your Frank a club joining type of man?'

'Plays golf and was talking about joining the sailing club,' Harriet said. 'He'll still be working though, so I'm not sure how much time he'll get down here. Besides, in theory, it is only for a year. We could decide to use it just as a holiday home afterwards.'

'Likely to happen?' Sabine said.

Harriet shrugged. 'Too soon to call it, but I have to admit I'm loving being back.' She sipped her champagne before saying, 'You ever thought of leaving?'

Sabine hesitated before nodding. 'Just the once.'

Sabine placed her glass on the small table and moved across to the bookshelves and took down the highly decorated wooden box.

'Pretty box,' Harriet said, looking at the boat and river scenes on it as Sabine took the lid off.

'Mmm,' Sabine said, picking out a photo. 'I painted it ages ago.' She handed Harriet the photo.

'Handsome man,' Harriet said. 'Who is he?'

'Reid Hamilton, a naval captain stationed over here years ago on some sort of exchange programme at the college.' Sabine held her hand out for the return of the photo and studied it sadly. 'He's the man who made me feel that there was a whole new world out there waiting to be explored – something I'd never felt before. I would have done anything to have gone away with him.'

'Why on earth didn't you go with him then? Oh – he was married?' Harriet said.

Sabine nodded. 'And so was I,' she added, putting the photo back in the box and placing it on the small table by her drink. 'It all happened a year before Dave died.'

She picked up her glass and took a long drink. 'It wasn't a full-blown affair – I never slept with him, although god knows I wanted to.'

'Did Dave ever know?'

Sabine shook her head. 'No. Nobody knew. Think Johnnie may have had his suspicions. You're the first person I've ever spoken to about Reid.'

'How long was he here?'

'Nine months. We met when he'd been here a fortnight. Owen introduced us. Ironic that, when you think about it.'

'So at the end of his assignment you kissed and waved each other goodbye?'

'Yes. Neither of us could bear the thought of hurting the people we were with – sounds old-fashioned these days, I know.' Sabine shrugged. 'That's just the way it was. The way we felt. We did give each other contact details and swore if we were ever free we'd get in touch.'

'So why didn't you contact him after Dave died?'

Sabine sighed. 'I didn't know what to do. I hadn't heard from him so I assumed he and his wife were still together. It was only a year after all and I didn't want to create a problem for him. In the end I cut the obituary notice out of the paper and sent it.' She twirled her glass around.

'I never heard anything back,' she said sadly. 'So I assumed he was still married. Haven't heard a word since to make me think it's changed. If it had, I know he would have come over. Told myself I'd wait a year after Dave died and then ring him.' She shook her head and looked at Harriet. 'But I never did.' She picked up the bottle of champagne and topped up both their glasses.

Both women were quiet for a minute, lost in their own thoughts as they sipped their drinks. It was Harriet who broke the silence.

'You still got the details?'

'Buried in the bottom of the box.'

'Must be sometime in the afternoon in America,' Harriet said.

Sabine glanced at her. 'You're not thinking ...'

'Yep. Seems like the perfect time. Give them to me and I'll do it on my mobile.'

'I'm not sure,' Sabine protested at the same time as she rifled through the box for the piece of paper. She looked at Harriet and then at the paper when she found it before handing it over. She took the photo out of the box again and studied it intently before saying, 'Oh what the hell. Go on then. If a woman answers, hang up immediately.'

In the time it took for Harriet to dial the number and the connection to be made, Sabine found herself holding her breath, not at all sure they should be doing this.

'I've put it on speaker,' Harriet said as the ringing tone filled the silence in the room.

The ringing tone stopped and a man's voice said, 'Hi. Reid here.'

'Reid Hamilton?' Harriet asked. Sabine nodded. She'd recognise that voice anywhere.

'Sure is. What can I do for you, honey?'

'I have someone here who would like to talk to you.' And Harriet handed the phone to a shaking Sabine.

'Hello, Reid. It's Sabine.'

Harriet picked up her glass and went downstairs. Some conversations needed absolute privacy.

Stunned, Sabine cut the connection and put Harriet's phone down on the table and sat for several moments, staring into space. She blinked rapidly in an effort to stop the tears falling as Harriet returned.

'I made us some hot chocolate,' Harriet said. 'Thought we might sleep better. Well? Is he catching the next

Virgin flight over?' She looked at her friend, waiting for her to speak.

Listlessly Sabine held her hand out for the mug. 'He's married,' she said.

'You knew that,' Harriet said gently.

'To his third wife,' Sabine said. Fifteen years of hoping that one day when he was free she and Reid would meet again all wasted. Instead, each time he'd been free he'd stayed in America and married someone else. 'Bastard.'

'Oh, Beeny, I'm so sorry.'

'Says he never received the obit notice about Dave. Didn't know I was a widow. Didn't take the trouble to find out though, did he, after his first divorce.' Sabine took a gulp of hot chocolate.

'He's been divorced twice? Never a widower?'

'Apparently not.'

'Not what you'd call good husband material then,' Harriet said.

Despite herself, Sabine smiled. 'Suppose not. Oh, Tatty, I've been such an idiot all these years, dreaming of him coming back to me when he was finally free.' How could she have been so stupid as to imagine he loved her enough to travel halfway across the world? 'Goes to show there's no fool like an old fool.'

'Hey, less of the old. We're women in the prime of life,' Harriet said. They looked at each other and laughed. 'Okay, maybe not the actual prime, but we're certainly not past our sell-by-date yet. Seriously, Beeny, you're better off knowing the truth even though it hurts.'

Sabine sniffed as she tore his photograph into bits of confetti. 'I know, but right now I'd like to castrate the bastard.'

Chapter Seventeen

Johnnie

Dawn was beginning to break as Johnnie steered Annie out to sea. A light sea mist was clinging to the hills and he could just make out the silhouettes of several cormorants on the Mewstone as they motored past. The wind, currently a light north-easterly, promised some good sailing for the next couple of hours.

Always an early riser, he loved the solitude this time of day offered out on the water – no distractions, just time to enjoy the quiet and, today, to think about what he was going to find when he got to France. Neither he nor Sabine had been able to work out what Martha's problem could possibly be.

The smell of bacon drifted up from the small galley where Rachel was busy making them breakfast and, no doubt, drinking a large mug of tea. An hour ago, when she'd arrived on the quay carrying a red kitbag she'd barely managed to mutter 'Good morning' as she'd stepped on board. 'Not a morning person, I'm afraid. Be all right when I've had some tea.'

Johnnie, feeling his spirits sag, hoped he'd done the right thing by inviting her to crew for him. The last thing he needed was some moody woman on board. He'd simply told her to put her stuff in the small cabin in the bow and then to come and help him cast off. To his relief she'd been more than competent with the ropes and within minutes they were underway, motoring out towards the mouth of the river.

'There's breakfast stuff in the galley. Want to go and rustle us up some food?' he said. 'I'll hoist the sails and we'll hove to for breakfast.' He realised he was being a tad chauvinistic, telling Rachel to do the cooking but no way was he prepared to hand the tiller to her until he knew how good a sailor she really was. She'd disappeared down into the cabin without a word.

Now, as he headed out into Start Bay, she reappeared with a large plate of bacon butties, two mugs of tea and, importantly, a smile on her face Johnnie was pleased to see.

'You awake now?' he asked.

Rachel nodded. 'Always need tea first thing. Didn't want to make a noise in the kitchen and disturb BB before I left.'

'He's settled in all right then?'

'Seems very happy. It's good having someone to keep an eye on the place while I'm away.' Rachel took a bite of her bacon sandwich. 'Mmm. Why does food always taste so much better when eaten at sea?' she said.

Johnnie didn't answer. He was too busy enjoying his own breakfast. He glanced at the main sail as it flapped in the wind.

'Think you've picked a good day for the trip,' Rachel said. 'Good steady wind.'

Johnnie nodded. 'We should make good time. Where were you based in the south of France?'

'Antibes.'

'Know it well. I've done a few deliveries down that way,' Johnnie said. 'So I guess you sailed mainly in the Med?'

Rachel nodded. 'France, Spain, Italy, Corsica, Malta. Places like that. The last couple of years we'd started to explore further east, but stopped when things began to get nasty over that way.'

'How big was your boat?'

'Last one was sixty foot. Hugo has it now. He has plans to charter it.'

'You miss your life down there?'

Rachel hesitated. 'If I'm truthful, yes. Although I'm really enjoying living in Dartmouth. I miss my husband though. He'd been ill so his death wasn't unexpected. It was still hard though, accepting it was all over.'

'It's the finality of it all, isn't it?' Johnnie said.

'This is the first time I've been sailing since he died,' Rachel said. 'I'm only now realising how big a part it played in my life and how much I'm missing it.' She finished her sandwich before glancing across at Johnnie and asking, 'Annie? What happened to her?'

'Big C,' Johnnie said briefly. 'Right – want to take the tiller for an hour?' It was too soon for them to have a conversation about Annie. There was no way he was going to discuss Annie and how much he missed her. Easier to change the subject and give Rachel the tiller.

'I'd love to.'

Over the following hours they settled into an easy on-board comradeship, both enjoying the sailing. Rachel prepared lunchtime cheese sandwiches which they ate sitting in the cockpit and afterwards they took it in turns at the tiller.

The wind was with them and they did make good time as Johnnie had predicted, arriving in Roscoff some eighteen hours later. Rachel got the sails down while Johnnie motored them into harbour. Once moored up, he took over culinary duties for their supper, heating up a ready meal and an apple tart.

Rachel, her offer of help having been declined, sat in the cockpit with a glass of wine looking out at the lights of the ancient town on the other side of the quay.

'Not high cuisine,' Johnnie said, joining her with plates of steaming risotto. 'Don't tell my French relatives how low I've sunk! At least the wine is a decent vintage!'

'Tell me about your French family,' Rachel said.

'Natives of Roscoff from time immemorial. Farming family and from the early twentieth century onion growers and exporters.'

'So how come you ended up on the other side of the channel?'

'Both Grandpapa and Papa were Johnny Onion boys,' Johnnie said. 'Travelling over to England every year to sell the onion harvest.'

'Oh I remember those from my childhood,' Rachel says. 'Bicycles loaded down with garlands of onions. There was a man who used to come to our small town every September. Always wore a striped shirt and a black beret. You could barely see his bicycle for onions. My mother always bought at least two large bunches. Swore they were the best onions she could buy.'

'That's them,' Johnnie said. 'By the fifties though the trade virtually died out. Which was when Papa met and married my Devonshire mother and settled in Dartmouth.' He drained his tea. 'Calling me Johnnie was his idea of reminding me where I came from. My sister got a proper French name though – Sabine LeRoy. Do you know her? She's Sabine Wills now. Runs the kiosk on the quay for the boat trips.'

Rachel caught her breath and choked before shaking her head. 'Sorry, something went down the wrong way.'

Johnnie looked at her, concerned for a minute, before saying, 'So where was this small town?' Johnnie asked.

'Small town? Oh where I grew up? Highbridge, Somerset. You've probably never heard of it.'

Before Johnnie could answer, Rachel finished the last of her wine and stifled a yawn before standing up. 'I'll just wash up and then I'll hit my bunk, if that's okay? Bit tired. Been a long day.' She picked up the plates as Johnnie went to help. 'No, you stay here and finish your wine. I'll see you in the morning. Goodnight, sleep well.'

'Goodnight and thanks for today's efforts,' Johnnie said, puzzled as to why she was making such a hasty retreat. What had he said?

Johnnie was already out on deck the next morning when Rachel surfaced. 'Kettle's boiled,' he called. 'Help yourself to a mug. Thought we'd have breakfast ashore today. Ready in fifteen?'

Johnnie led the way to a small cafe down a side street that was busy with fishermen and sailors all enjoying versions of the local speciality, crepes.

While they were waiting for their crepes to arrive, Johnnie said, 'Would you like to come with me and meet Cousin Martha?'

Rachel instantly shook her head. 'I wouldn't dream of intruding on a family problem. Besides, I'm really looking forward to having a wander around Roscoff.'

'Okay. You'd better take these then.' And he pushed the keys to Annie's cockpit hatch across the table to her. 'Just so you can at least get inside if you want to. I shouldn't be too long. I'm hoping we'll be able to catch the next tide.'

Rachel picked the keys up and put them in her bag without a word. Johnnie opened his mouth to say something but the waitress arrived with their coffee and crepes and the moment was lost.

Apart from a muttered 'delicious' from Rachel, breakfast was eaten in silence and finished quickly. Johnnie pushed his chair back and stood up. Placing a twenty-euro note on the table, he said, 'Okay, I'll see you back at the boat. Shouldn't be too long.'

Walking through town to Martha's, Johnnie thought about the difference twelve hours had made in Rachel. Yesterday he'd thought they were getting along fine, enjoying the sailing and each other's company, but then during supper, the shutters had come down. Today there was a definite chill in the air between them.

It was almost as if Rachel had decided not to talk to him. Damned if he could figure out why. Get this business at Martha's sorted and on their return trip he'd try to get her to tell him what had upset her so badly.

The front door to Martha's terraced cottage was unlocked and he gave a quick knock before calling out, 'Martha, *J'arrive*,' and walking in.

'Finally you're here,' Martha said as they kissed cheeks when he found her in the small conservatory at the back of the house.

'So tell me, what's the problem? Oh, who's this?' Johnnie said, seeing a small girl in a buggy. Martha had numerous grandchildren but he didn't remember seeing one this young for some time.

'Hello, who are you?' he said to the child, who simply sucked her thumb and stared at him.

'She's Carla,' Martha said before adding quietly, 'And she's all yours.'

'Hello, Carla, I'm John …' He swung round to face Martha. 'What the hell do you mean, she's all mine?'

Chapter Eighteen

Sabine

'Just a few places left for tomorrow's river trip, folks,' Sabine said as a group of holidaymakers walked past the kiosk. 'Don't miss out.' She smiled as they shook their heads and carried on. Couldn't win them all.

Inside the kiosk she switched the kettle on. Time for a coffee. While she waited for the kettle to boil, she checked the bookings spreadsheet on her laptop. Bookings were slightly up on last year and there were also a few more private parties booked for Owen's other boat, Daughter of the River, with its dance floor in the saloon and catering facilities. Tonight there was a twenty-first birthday party on board for fifty people.

Sipping her coffee, Sabine watched as Daughter, already alongside the pontoon, was loaded with the evening's supply of champagne and food. Watching Peter as he helped the suppliers carry stuff on board, she wondered how Trevor Bagshawe was getting on with sorting out the legal stuff. Owen had said it would take a few weeks and then he planned to take them both for a slap-up dinner and break the news to Peter.

'What is it you English say? A penny for your thoughts?' BB asked, appearing at her side and making her jump.

'Oh hi, BB. I was miles away. How are you?' Sabine said.

'Great. Just great. Thanks to Johnnie I've found a room in an old cottage and while the landlady is away for a few days, I've got the place to myself.'

'I'm pleased for you. Any news on the relatives?'

'Not yet,' BB said. 'It's frustrating and fascinating at the same time! I've kind of got hooked too on researching the history of this place rather than looking for any cousins. I bet you have no idea how many people called Seale or Holdsworth lived in this town back in the day. Sadly, none of the ones I've found so far appear to be my ancestors. Right, I'm off to the marina to talk boats. Don't suppose Johnnie is around?'

'No, he's in France. Should be back tomorrow or the day after if you want his advice. Before you go, scrawl your signature on the Save the Kiosk petition, will you?' she said, handing him a pen.

'Sure thing.'

Watching BB stroll off in the direction of the marina, Sabine's thoughts turned to Johnnie. Had he sorted out whatever the problem had turned out to be over in Roscoff? He hadn't phoned, which was unusual when he was visiting Martha. Normally he'd ring to ask was there anything she wanted brought back apart from the inevitable sack of onions. This time, when she'd planned to ask him to pick up a Kouign-amann as a special treat from the award-winning patisserie near the harbour, he hadn't rung. Probably just as well really, there was no doubt the delicious butter-laden gateau posed a serious threat to her waistline.

A harassed-looking Owen arrived late afternoon as she was unhooking her pictures from the open door and preparing to close up for the day.

'Any chance you can help out tonight? Caterers have said they're short staffed.'

'I've told Tristan I'd start to get my pictures down to him tonight,' Sabine said. 'He wants to start planning where to hang them for next week's exhibition. It'll take me a couple of hours.'

'Work tonight and I'll give you a hand in the morning,' Owen said. 'I can carry more than you at a time so be quicker anyway.'

'Okay. I'll take a couple of the smaller ones down to him and tell him we'll take the rest down tomorrow morning early. What time?'

'Casting off at 7 so about 6.30. Thanks, you're a life-saver. See you later.'

Early evening and after taking three of the smaller pictures into Tristan at the gallery and promising the rest for the morning, Sabine walked on towards the quay and Daughter of the River.

It wasn't often Owen asked her to help out with on-board functions, but when he did she quite enjoyed it. The party atmosphere of tonight's do promised a few hours of fun and mind-numbing disco music to help her forget how stupid she still felt over Reid. All those wasted years yearning for someone who proved to be unobtainable in the end.

Daughter of the River was dressed overall, its coloured lights casting pools of shimmering reflections the length of the boat in the river water. As she walked up the gangplank, Sabine could hear the muted sounds of disco music pulsating down in the saloon as the night's DJ ran a sound check.

She was kept busy for the next couple of hours, handing champagne to guests as they arrived, helping keep the buffet tables topped up with food and then, as guests drifted up to the main deck to watch the sun set over Dartmouth, giving a hand with the clearing up.

It was ten o'clock before the woman in charge turned to her and said, 'Thanks, Sabine. Any time you want to leave that old kiosk, let me know. I'll give you a job any time.'

Sabine smiled, but before she could say anything, Owen's voice behind her said, 'Hands off my staff, missus. Find your own.'

She turned to face him as he said, 'I've left Peter in charge in the wheelhouse. Join me on deck for a drink?' He waved a bottle of wine and two glasses at her.

Sabine took a deep breath of the cool night air as she followed Owen outside, the deck beneath their feet vibrating with the loud music.

'Lively party,' she said, leaning against the rail. 'Remember when we were twenty-one? Our whole lives still before us. Everything still possible.'

Owen poured the wine as he answered her. 'All those wrong decisions still waiting to be made.' He handed her a glass. 'Cheers.'

'Cheers,' Sabine echoed as they clinked glasses. 'Come on, Owen. Your life hasn't turned out that badly, has it?' Fleetingly she thought of her own life. Giving up her art college place was top of her 'mistakes I have made in life' list, but that was a decision life itself had taken for her. She'd never have forgiven herself if she hadn't been there for Mum. And then there was Reid. Best not think about that particular mistake.

'No, it's not bad at all but ...' Owen sighed. 'I don't know. Sometimes I feel I should have been more assertive over certain things. Rebelled a bit. Stood up to Dad.' He took a large drink of wine. 'Had a bit more backbone and fought for my dreams instead of always taking the easy option and drifting into things. I might even have got married and had a family then.'

'Is this what your six months travelling is really all about?' Sabine asked quietly.

Owen nodded. 'Yes. Something just for me. You thought any more about coming?'

'Depends. I'd really like to see places like Mexico, America, China, India, you know places like that as well as just Europe.'

'We can do that,' Owen said instantly. 'Go to the far-flung places first and work our way back to Europe. Sorted!'

Sabine laughed. 'When exactly did I say yes to coming with you?'

'Oh come on, Sabine, stop teasing,' Owen said, putting his arm around her shoulders and squeezing her. 'You know you want to come. We'll have a ball. Just say yes.'

Chapter Nineteen

BB

Standing in the bow of the Dartmouth Princess passenger ferry as it left the Kingswear pontoon and made its way across the river, BB closed his eyes momentarily, enjoying the feel of the wind against his face and the smell of the tangy salt air. After a day spent in Exeter library researching papers he'd been unable to access on the Internet, it was good to stand out in the fresh air. It was good too, to feel the movement of a boat under his feet. He really must start some serious yacht hunting soon or the summer would disappear and he'd have literally missed the boat. The only boats he'd been offered so far hadn't been ideal. Next time he saw Johnnie, he'd ask if he'd heard about anything suitable on his travels.

As the ferry's warning hooter sounded, BB opened his eyes and, looking up river, he saw a sailing yacht urgently changing tack to get out of the path of the advancing ferry. The Naval College high on the bank, its red bricks illuminated in the evening sunlight, brought Grandpa Randy and Uncle Lance to mind. He knew now they would both have set foot there while it was the wartime HQ for the US Navy.

He also knew from the several black-and-white photographs he'd seen in the museum that the river then had been full of various naval vessels and landing-craft, all involved in Operation Overlord; preparing for the D-Day assault across the channel. Other photos had shown the town itself had been extra busy too, with every available space taken up. Coronation Park, out of bounds to the locals, had been covered with a multitude of Nissen huts, workshops and tanks – all the paraphernalia of a world war.

Standing on the ferry watching all the peaceful modern-day activity on the river, it was hard to conjure up a picture of the grimness of the earlier era. It was a sobering thought to think Randy and Lance had travelled three thousand miles to this place when it had been the nerve centre of a war campaign. Strangers in a country who would forever be a part of the history of this place, particularly Lance who'd never made it back home. Killed in the E-boat debacle out at Torcross, April 1944.

Leaving the ferry, he walked into town to buy an early takeaway supper of fish and chips before taking a short cut up Browns Hill Steps to Rachel's cottage. Five minutes later, he was out on the small terrace, enjoying his supper with a glass of red wine and looking forward to spending the evening doing yet more research on the Internet.

Today he'd learnt even more about the Holdsworth and the Seale families historically, but still hadn't uncovered much information about any twentieth-century families with those surnames. Tonight he planned to log onto a site the librarian at Exeter had given him the details of that apparently had the birth, marriage and death records from the three Dartmouth churches. Surely he'd find Grandma Mary's baptism details recorded there and possible links to her family?

An hour later, the dining room table was covered with papers and notebooks as he attempted to make some sense out of the things both his library and Internet research had discovered. This genealogy business sure was complicated. It didn't help matters either that so many sons were named after their fathers – whole generations of similar names. BB had lost count of the number of Johns in the Seale family records. Holdsworth records were as bad with the name Arthur. Now though, he was sure of one thing: both these families had been the kingpins of Dartmouth a couple of centuries ago. The fact that he'd discovered a long-running feud had existed between them was beginning to add even more interest to his research.

He couldn't resist triumphantly waving his fist in the air when he found Grandma Mary Seale's christening date in St Saviour's church – Sunday 19th April 1925. At last he was getting somewhere.

Intriguingly Mary's mother had been one Amelia Holdsworth before she married William Seale. Given the rivalry he now knew had existed between the two families, he'd guess that particular union hadn't been greeted with delight.

He sighed and rubbed his eyes. As fascinating as these old records were, he'd had enough for the evening and he bookmarked the last page ready for the next day before he closed the site down. Before he could shut down the laptop completely, the Skype connection began buzzing.

'Hi, Jess, how's things?'

'Great. You?' Without waiting for an answer, Jess continued. 'You know that box of old stuff from Grandma Mary I've been going through with Mom? Turns out most of the stuff is Uncle Lance's that Grandpa Randy couldn't bear to throw away.'

'Anything interesting?'

'There's a photo of him and a woman and a half-written letter to someone he calls 'My Darling Florrie' whom I presume is the woman in the photo. They look very happy together. There's a few other papers all in an official army envelope – guess its stuff they returned when he was killed. Haven't had time to look at those properly yet.'

'Sure sounds like it. I don't suppose there's an address on the half-finished letter for this Florrie, is there?'

'Sorry, no. Want me to post it and the photo over to you?'

'Be quicker if you scan them first, plus anything else interesting you find, and email them to me. I can print out copies then. Show the picture around – see if any of the older generation recognise her.'

'Okay, will do.'

'Mom okay?'

'Yeah. Missing the golden boy though! You might try ringing her sometime! She'd prefer that to your emails.'

BB sighed. 'I do think about ringing and then realise it's in the middle of the night with the time difference. Is she there now? You could put her on.'

'Nope, she's gone to a seniors' tea party. I'll give her your love. Got to go.'

BB opened up his laptop early the next morning, hoping Jessie had scanned the photo and the letter, but was disappointed to find his mailbox folder empty. He opened the website he'd bookmarked the previous evening and started to scroll down through the pages of records relating to St Saviour's.

He was becoming more and more convinced that Grandma Mary's Dartmouth family had simply died out and there were no long-lost cousins waiting to be discovered. Five minutes later, he found himself staring at the screen, trying to make sense of an entry he was reading on a page dated Sunday 28th January 1945.

Chapter Twenty

Johnnie

Johnnie was still staring at Martha, waiting for her to answer when the conservatory door was pushed open.

'Hello, Johnnie,' a soft voice said. 'Martha's right. Carla is yours.'

Johnnie spun round. 'Josette?'

Josette, a slender woman in her mid-thirties, had always reminded him of a younger Annie with her big brown eyes and a determined attitude to life from the day they'd met. Even though he knew she was much too young for him, at a time when he'd been in desperate need of someone to love him, it hadn't seemed to matter. Had even been a part of the attraction.

'I'll take Carla for a walk in the park,' Martha said. 'You two can talk in private.' She began to push the buggy and Carla out of the room.

'Martha, wait a moment, please,' Josette said, before bending over to gently kiss Carla. 'Enjoy the park, sweetie. Be a good girl. Mama loves you.' Straightening up, she blinked rapidly as Martha wheeled the buggy out of the room.

'You absolutely sure she's mine?' Johnnie winced at the look Josette gave him. 'Sorry. Insensitive.' Hell, he'd already seen the resemblance for himself. The LeRoy traits were all there on the baby's face – from the dimple in the chin, the set of the eyes, to the mole high on the left cheek like his.

'So is this about maintenance? Fine. How much?'

Josette shook her head. 'No. I've been managing quite well on my own, thank you. Besides, it's too late for that.' She took a deep breath before saying, 'I'm giving her to you.'

Stunned, Johnnie felt his mouth drop open. 'You what?'

'I've met someone. He wants me to marry him and move to Paris but …' She stopped, her voice cracking. 'He refuses to take Carla as well.' She looked at him pleadingly.

'Johnnie, please take her and give her a good life. I know you'll be a wonderful father. I've finally got the chance to leave here and have a proper life of my own. If you don't take her I'm stuck forever – or at least until she's grown up and then it will be too late anyway.' She brushed a tear away. 'You told me how much you and your wife wanted a child, well now you've got one.'

'*Merde*. I don't believe this is happening. How old is she?' Johnnie said, distractedly rubbing the back of his neck.

'Nine months.'

'Why didn't you tell me you were pregnant?'

'Remember the last time we saw each other?' she said quietly.

Johnnie nodded. 'Of course.' They'd had a lovely evening, ending up at her small apartment where he'd plucked up the courage to gently tell her that it was the last time. There could be no future in their relationship. He was too old for her.

That was what? Seventeen months ago? He'd only seen her once since then in the distance when she'd waved a hand at him in acknowledgement and hurried away before he could catch up with her.

'I was going to tell you then but instead you told me it was over. That you were too old for me. I did think about telling you then anyway, but couldn't face the thought you might accuse me of lying about being on the pill. Of trying to trap you.'

Josette pulled a tissue out of her jacket pocket, struggling to keep her tears in check. 'If it's any consolation, I had decided I'd tell you on her first birthday. I wanted you to at least know you had a daughter. But meeting Herve has changed things for me.'

Johnnie stayed silent, waiting.

'I've gone over and over in my mind what is the best thing to do – for her, for me. I can't stay living here when the alternative is out there for me to take. If that makes me selfish ...' Josette shrugged, but the next moment she turned on him. 'Don't ever think I don't love her because I do, and don't even for one minute think I'm taking the easy route by handing her over to you. I'm not.'

Johnnie regarded her steadily. 'I don't think that. Even if I start paying maintenance and make regular visits, you won't stay, will you?'

Josette shook her head. 'No. You'll grow to love your daughter, but you don't love me. Herve, on the other hand, does love me and is waiting for me in Paris.

'Will you please talk to her about me? I can't bear the thought of her not knowing about me. Tell her how much I love her. I'll keep in touch with you and Martha so you can send me photos and things. I'll send her presents too, if that's okay with you? Perhaps I can visit occasionally?'

'So not a complete break, then?' Johnnie said. 'Tell me: what happens if it all goes wrong with Herve and you return? You going to want to take her back? I tell you now, if you leave her with me I shall get official custody to make sure she stays with me. Messing her about is not on. Even I know children require stability in their lives.'

Josette smiled wanly. 'I promise I'll never demand you return her to me. She's a shared responsibility between the two of us, but you get to do the fun full-on day-to-day stuff for the next eighteen years. Right.' She took a deep breath. 'There's everything you need there,' she said, pointing to a suitcase and two large bags in the corner of the room Johnnie hadn't even noticed.

'Nappies, jars of baby food, milk powder, clothes, toys etc., etc.' She delved into her bag. 'Better put these somewhere safe.' And she handed him a passport and a birth certificate.

'I'm leaving for Paris this evening. I'll go now before Martha gets back with Carla.'

Seeing the tears glistening in her eyes, Johnnie sighed before pulling her towards him and hugging her. 'I promise I'll take good care of her.'

Josette kissed his cheek. 'I know you will, otherwise I wouldn't give her to you. One last thing, don't ever tell her she was a mistake. We might not ever have been "in love", but we were lovers for a short time.'

The door banged behind her and she was gone.

Left alone, Johnnie swore loudly, '*Merde!*'

He was still standing there, dazed, trying to make sense of the situation, when Martha returned with Carla asleep in the buggy.

In that moment, the reality of his situation hit him. Josette had literally left him holding the baby.

'She's gone then?' Martha said.

Johnnie nodded. 'I wish you'd warned me what I was coming over to.'

'Josette asked me not to. She was afraid you wouldn't come if you knew what she planned. She's not done this lightly,' Martha said. 'She knows you won't let Carla or her down.'

'I'm a yacht deliverer, for god's sake – I'm away for days, weeks sometimes. How the hell am I expected to cope with this … child?' He gesticulated at the sleeping baby.

'Carla's a sweetie. You'll find a way of coping.'

'Any chance you could keep her here if I pay you? No, forget it. I shouldn't even be thinking like that,' Johnnie said, running his hands through his hair.

'You and Annie always wanted a child, well, now you've got one,' Martha said gently, echoing Josette's earlier words.

'I wanted a child with Annie,' Johnnie said. 'Not with a woman I barely know.'

Chapter Twenty-One

Rachel

After Johnnie left the cafe to go to his cousin's, Rachel ordered herself another cup of coffee and sipped it thoughtfully. Over the months since she'd been back in Dartmouth, she'd grown used to being economical with the truth. Used to mixing with incomers rather than the true locals. Used to shopping in the newer shops with their younger assistants. When people asked her about her past, or where she was from originally, she never named anything or anywhere specific. Never gave them any encouragement to ask more questions. Last night she'd broken her golden rule by telling Johnnie where she grew up.

The wine and the growing intimacy between the two of them had been her downfall, lulling her into forgetting the need to be careful. The need to keep her guilty secret hidden from nosey parkers. Not that Johnnie LeRoy fell into that category. He seemed a genuinely nice man. A sexy one too.

Maybe it hadn't been such a good idea to come on this trip. Being back on board a yacht again though was good. She'd thoroughly enjoyed the sail over and had been looking forward to the journey back. Now she couldn't wait to get it over with. Their friendship had to stop before it had really begun. There would be no more crewing for him or sharing a coffee in The Royal, that was for sure.

After paying the breakfast bill and leaving the cafe, Rachel wandered around the town. She was glad Johnnie had elected to use the old harbour rather than the new marina just outside of town. It did at least give her a chance to explore somewhere she'd never been before. Beautiful granite and historical buildings were everywhere, many decorated with baskets full of red, white and blue flowers.

Scattered amongst the usual touristy shops with their postcards and souvenir items, there were art galleries, bistros, jewellers, takeaway food shops and boutiques selling nautical-influenced clothes. There was even Celtic music drifting out of an open window to add to the atmosphere.

From the tabac, Rachel bought a postcard with various views of Roscoff on it, quickly addressed it to Hugo before scrawling across it, 'Surprise! Sailed across the Channel yesterday! Love, Mum.'

Slipping the card into the yellow post box on the wall, Rachel glanced at her watch. Nearly twelve o'clock. Better return to Annie in case Johnnie returned and wanted to get down to his cabin. Sitting on deck in the sunshine with her Kindle would pass the time if he wasn't back yet.

At one o'clock, when he still hadn't returned, she made herself a sandwich and a cup of tea and settled herself in the cockpit to eat. Clearly Johnnie's family business must have been more difficult to deal with than anticipated – he'd been gone for four hours now.

Eating her lunch, Rachel watched the activity in the harbour, something she'd done many times before in various harbours in the south when Hugo and his father had gone off on some errand or other. Watching a fishing vessel return to its mooring, squawking gulls circling above, the smell of fish and diesel mixed together drifting on the wind reminded her more of Dartmouth and its crab boats returning from Start Bay though rather than Antibes in the south of France.

Unlike Antibes, there wasn't a single large yacht of the floating gin palace variety in the harbour as far as she could see whereas Antibes with its millionaire quay was a veritable honeypot of international, foreign-registered boats flying the flag of their tax haven registered country.

A few of the private yachts in the harbour here were flying the English red ensign, but in the main the boats were French registered and flying the French flag. If there were any super-yachts up here in this channel port, they were all probably moored against the pontoons in the new marina with its 'Capitaine' and twenty-four-hour security.

It was mid-afternoon before Rachel saw Johnnie marching along the quay towards her.

Carrying two large carrier bags and pulling a suitcase, he wasn't, judging by his body language, in the best of moods. Rachel eyed him warily. And who was the woman pushing a child in a buggy at his side?

'Rachel, meet my Cousin Martha,' Johnnie said, placing the two bags on Annie's deck before heaving the suitcase on board.

'We've got a passenger for the trip back,' he said.

'Pleased to meet you, Martha,' Rachel said. 'Welcome aboard.'

'Martha's not coming,' Johnnie said.

'So who is?' Rachel asked, surprised.

'Carla,' Johnnie said as Martha unbuckled the safety harness and handed the child to him before folding up the buggy.

Rachel, stunned into silence, could only watch as he carefully climbed on board holding Carla tightly. She looked at Martha, hoping the woman would give her a clue as to what was going on but only got a shrug in response, followed by a sympathetic smile.

'Johnnie, just think what Annie would want you to do. You'll cope. Give Sabine my love. See you next trip. Pleasure to meet you, Rachel,' and she was gone.

'You look a bit shell-shocked,' Rachel said quietly. 'Give me Carla. I'll hold her while you get things down into the cabin.'

'Thanks. Then if it's okay with you, I think we'll start back. Going to be a long haul – wind's not right.'

Rachel nodded. 'Fine by me.' The wind was not the only thing that was not right, that was for sure. Johnnie's stiff body language as he sorted ropes and prepared to cast off was speaking volumes. He was clearly one unhappy man. Would he talk to her on the way home? Or would he do the British stiff upper lip thing, bottle everything up and pretend everything was under control?

Chapter Twenty-Two

Harriet

'Mum. Dad. Wait!' Ellie shouted, coming out of the house as Harriet was about to get into Frank's car, waving her mobile in the air.

'What's the matter?'

'I've just got a commission to do a feature on a new hotel opening in Bath. They want me there on Thursday for a day or two. Means I won't get down to you in time for your friend's exhibition opening.'

'But you were going to write a piece about it,' Harriet said, smothering her dismay. The thought 'And I was going to tell to you about the legacy and ... things' ran through her mind. And what about the latest letter from Trevor Bagshawe, asking her and her daughter to make an appointment to see him ASAP now that the legal stuff was sorted and ready for signatures. That in part was what this 'family holiday' break she'd persuaded Ellie to come on was all about really. Of course she hadn't told her the real reason behind it, but time was rapidly running out to tell Ellie the truth. And yet more lies had been added into the deceit of decades. Now it was all falling apart.

'I know, sorry about that. The thing is, I don't have a commission for that whereas this I do and I need the money. I'll get there before it finishes though and still write a piece about the exhibition, like I promised, and try to find a home for it,' Ellie said. 'I'm sure your friend will understand.'

Knowing there was nothing she could do, Harriet sighed. 'Okay. We'll see you when we see you.' And she got in the car.

Frank glanced at her. 'Best-laid plans and all that.'

'Hmmm,' Harriet said, before muttering a swear word under her breath.

'You still want a lift to the station?'

'Yes, of course. Why wouldn't I? Ellie thinks I'm coming with you on a business trip and then we're going on down to Dartmouth together. She didn't know I was going there on my own first to finish preparing things.'

'Just thought you might like to stay and talk to Ellie here.'

Harriet shook her head vehemently. 'Definitely not. I want to do it in situ, so to speak.' Superstitiously she felt telling Ellie about the legacy and everything had to be done in Dartmouth. In Amy's house. Everything would be all right if she talked to Ellie there. The spirit of Amy would soothe the hurt that Ellie was sure to feel over the deceit. Ridiculous? Maybe, but that's how she felt and how she intended to do it. She simply had to be in Dartmouth, in the house itself, when she told Ellie everything.

Letting herself into the house later that day after the taxi ride from Totnes station, Harriet heaved a sigh. It felt good to be back. Living here for a year wasn't going to be the hardship she'd feared, although there was still the little problem of Ellie's reaction to everything. Trying to second-guess just how she would react was an utter waste of time. She could only pray that Ellie would realise that everything, everything they'd done in the past, had been done out of love and the desire to protect her.

Making herself a cup of tea, she took it through to the sitting room and drank it standing in front of the large French doors, watching the activity on the river. A bank of large rhododendron bushes and a holly tree were blocking the view somewhat and she made a note to get Frank to trim them back over the weekend.

With the house cleaned and polished from top to bottom, apart from the locked studio, which she was deliberately ignoring as having too much of Amy's personal stuff in there to cope with yet, the garden would be her project for summer. Maybe Ellie would like her thirtieth birthday party here? It was a superb setting with its river views and the twin castles visible at the mouth of the estuary. Amy had held some wonderful parties here in the past with the garden transformed into a fairy-tale place with garden lights and candles everywhere, soft music playing in the background.

Amy's friends were an eclectic bunch and it had always amazed Harriet how they all fitted seamlessly into the party spirit. Anywhere else they would surely have been at loggerheads with each other. The last party she'd attended here had been different, of course. It was the evening her life, as she'd known it, had started to unravel.

Harriet remembered she was wearing a summer dress with bunches of cherries all over it the evening of the party. Definitely not high fashion, but a dress she'd always felt comfortable wearing. Oscar, in his trademark attire of jeans and a white shirt buckled at the waist with his wide leather belt, honey-coloured cashmere sweater slung over his shoulders, faded blue deck shoes on his feet, had looked what he was: a sexy, successful man.

A last-minute hitch with a babysitter for Ellie had meant she and Oscar had arrived half an hour after the party had begun. Amy had immediately swept them out into the garden, saying there was somebody whom 'you absolutely must meet. I know you'll be great friends'.

Sabine, glass of wine in her hand, and standing under the wisteria-covered pergola talking to an unknown woman, waved them over the moment she saw them. 'Tatty, Oscar, meet Vanessa.'

Oscar, once the introductions had been made, said he needed a word with Dave and left the three women to chat. At the time she'd been surprised by how quickly he'd left the three of them. It wasn't until later that Harriet realised just how hasty his retreat had been. How desperate he'd been to put distance between himself and Vanessa.

Listening to Sabine and Vanessa progress from small talk to genuine getting-to-know-each-other questions, Harriet sensed how much they liked each other with an instant rapport springing up between them. Usually she and Beeny were on the same wavelength as far as friends went, but strangely this time she didn't feel a scrap of empathy with this self-contained women and her air of quiet competence, as friendly as she appeared to be. But Beeny liked her, so she tried.

'How long have you been in town?' she'd asked.

'Me? A month. Tom came down on his own eight weeks ago. Bit of an emergency replacement for his predecessor who had to retire early due to illness. No idea how long we'll be here. Might be a permanent position.' Vanessa shrugged. 'Might not. Secretly, I hope we stay. I love it here.'

'Bit of a trouble-shooter is he, your husband?' Beeny said. 'Is he here tonight?'

'Trouble-shooting is as good an expression as any for what he does 24/7,' Vanessa said, laughing. 'And no, he's not here yet.' She glanced at her watch. 'I'll introduce you when he gets here.'

But she never did introduce Harriet to her husband. An hour or so later, when music was floating over the garden from the CDs Amy had put on encouraging people to dance, Harriet went in search of Oscar, determined to get him to dance, something he always professed to hate. Finding him and Vanessa dancing intimately together in a dark corner of the garden tore her world apart.

By the time Tom Harford arrived, Harriet had invented an emergency call home from an anxious babysitter, made her apologies to Amy and left.

It was a month before she and Tom Harford came face to face. The day he came to talk to her about his wife and her husband's affair. That was the day the dress with the cherries went in the bin. She couldn't bear the thought of wearing it again. It would be forever associated with the evening at Amy's in her mind.

Harriet shook herself. No point in going over old ground. Best to chalk it up to experience and forget it. Thirty years on, life was good, she and Sabine were best friends again, she was about to move back to Dartmouth and once the three of them had had the planned talk, it would be a good summer.

Up early the next morning, she walked around the garden working out a master plan for getting it back into shape. The shrubs would all benefit from a good pruning, as would the roses around the small summer house in the corner. The wisteria over the pergola appeared to have died. Good. The pergola could stay but she'd buy a different vine to clamber up and over it.

Two hours later, she was busy tackling an overgrown border and pulling forget-me-nots out by the bucketload when the large ship's brass bell Amy had hung outside the front door years ago shattered the silence.

'Can't hear a normal doorbell when I'm in the garden,' Amy had said when the bell had first appeared. 'Be hard to miss this though. Loud enough to wake the dead in St Petrox churchyard.' Amy had grinned wickedly, no doubt anticipating the complaints that were sure to come from her more alive neighbours.

Down the years it certainly hadn't lost any of its exuberant tone, Harriet thought as she made her way up the garden path.

A youngish man dressed in a suit and looking mildly embarrassed at the noise he'd created was standing on the drive looking around.

'Can I help you?'

'I'm looking for Miss James.'

Harriet shook her head. 'Sorry. No-one here of that name.'

'Are you sure? This is definitely the address I was given by the office.'

Harriet looked at him. 'This is my house so, yes, I'm reasonably sure no-one of that name lives here. Your office must have given you the wrong information.'

Something stopped her as she went to return to the garden and she looked again at the young man who'd made no attempt to leave. Better check out his credentials at least. He didn't look like he was casing the place, but then who knew what would-be burglars looked like?

'Who are you anyway?'

'Nick Walters. Literary agent.' He took a card out of his pocket and handed it to her.

Harriet glanced at it before asking, 'This Miss James you're looking for is an author then?'

Nick nodded. 'One of our most popular ones. And this is definitely the address I was told.'

Harriet looked at him thoughtfully. 'Well, there's definitely no-one here of that name, but would you like a cup of coffee?'

For some reason she had a niggling feeling she needed to talk to this man. 'Maybe we can work out why you were given this address.'

'Thanks,' Nick said and followed her into the house.

Once the coffee was on, Harriet said, 'My daughter and I have recently inherited this house from an Amy Widdicombe who lived here for, oh, forty years I suppose. So I really don't see where your Miss James comes in.'

'This is the address all Cassandra James's letters and contracts have been sent to since the agency has acted for her.'

'Have you ever met her?'

'Yes. She always attended our yearly author parties. Normally we—'

'Hang on a minute,' Harriet interrupted. 'Did you say Cassandra James?'

'Yes. Why?'

'There's shelves full of books by that author in the study.' Harriet took the study key off its hook before saying, 'Follow me. This is the one room in the house I haven't touched yet, but maybe I should have paid more attention to it.'

Nick looked at the shelf of Cassandra James books, the folders on the desk, the piles of books on the floor, before pointing to a photograph and saying, 'Is that your Amy?'

'Yes.'

'In that case, I have to tell you, Amy Widdicombe and Cassandra James are one and the same woman.' He moved across to the desk. 'May I switch the computer on?'

'Feel free,' Harriet said. Amy a successful novelist? Well, she certainly hadn't seen that one coming although maybe if she'd cleared the studio she would have discovered it for herself. At least the mystery of where all Amy's money had come from was solved.

'How many books had she written?' Harriet asked.

'Forty-five. Most of them were translated into various languages too.' He clicked on an icon. 'Look, here's the folder with the forty-sixth unfinished one.'

'So what happens now?' Harriet said.

'I'll notify the office and then … then I honestly don't know what happens. It's the first time I've ever had an author die on me,' Nick said.

'Trevor Bagshawe, the solicitor here in town, has been dealing with Amy's estate. If you contact him I'm sure he'll know what has to happen next,' Harriet said. 'I wonder if he knew Amy's secret?'

Perhaps that was what he intended to talk to Ellie about at her appointment when Harriet had told her the truth about the house and her inheritance.

Chapter Twenty-Three

Johnnie

Johnnie automatically went through the routine of getting the yacht safely out of harbour and setting the course for home. Despite his best efforts though, he couldn't silence the thoughts swirling around his brain.

How the hell was he, a single man with no experience of children, going to deal with having a baby in his life? A baby that even as he hoisted Annie's main sail, was letting her presence be known with a series of high-pitched cries.

He knew he was being chauvinistic – again – by simply leaving Rachel to deal with the child, but right now he couldn't face it himself. He needed time to try to begin to come to terms with the events of the last twelve hours. No wonder Martha had been evasive in her letter and on the phone when she'd urged him to visit ASAP. Would he have gone had she told him there was a child involved?

Yes, of course he would. He wasn't one of those men who shirked their responsibility. He would have readily paid Josette maintenance from day one if only she'd told him. Provided for the child to the best of his ability. He'd never have stood by and seen them struggling financially, but having complete responsibility thrust on him in this way was a shock and would take some accepting.

Jumping down into the cockpit, he realised the cries had stopped. A quick glance inside the saloon and he saw Rachel patiently spoon-feeding Carla from one of the jars Josette had provided.

'Where do you want her to sleep tonight?' Rachel asked, seeing him standing there.

'Anywhere. Does it matter?'

'Of course it matters. Has to be somewhere she can't roll out of for a start.' Rachel sighed. 'Don't worry. I'll sort something for her.'

It was another hour before Rachel joined him on deck and handed him a glass of wine. 'I'm sure you need this as much as I do.'

'Thanks. It's quiet down there.'

Rachel nodded. 'She's asleep. I made up a bed for her on the floor of the small cabin in the end with the cushions from the aft bunk. At least she can't fall out and I've padded the sides with more cushions so even if she rolls over she shouldn't hurt herself.'

'Want to take the tiller over while I get some food?' Johnnie asked.

'Thought you'd never ask,' Rachel said.

Before he started on the food, Johnnie went forward to take a look at Carla. The little girl was sleeping peacefully on her back, one arm across her chest with the pink rabbit she'd been holding the first time he'd set eyes on her clutched tightly to her and the thumb of her other hand firmly in her mouth.

Johnnie felt his heart contract as he looked at her. Poor little mite. None of this was her fault. Gently he knelt down and kissed her cheek.

'Worry not, little one. I promise to look after you.' Standing up, he was surprised to find his eyes suspiciously moist and he wiped them dry with the back of his hand before returning to the tiny galley.

Waiting for the water to boil before adding pasta and heating the Bolognese sauce, Johnnie thought about the future for him and Carla. Would it just be the two of them for the next few years with the occasional visit from Josette? He'd believed her when she'd told him she'd no intention of walking out of Carla's life totally, that she was trying to do the best thing for her. How would she react though if he met someone and they became Carla's step-mum? Mentally he shook himself as he drained the pasta water down the sink. Realistically, what woman was going to look at him with the baggage he'd acquired in the last few hours?

Sitting together in the cockpit eating the steaming plates of spaghetti Bolognese, Rachel looked at him before saying, 'Tell me to mind my own business if you like, but I'm a good listener if you want to talk about things.'

'I'm sorry you've got caught up in all this,' Johnnie said. 'I'd never have suggested you crew for me if I'd known this was going to happen.'

Rachel shrugged. 'I'm glad I'm here to help.'

There was silence for several minutes while they both concentrated on their food before Johnnie, feeling Rachel was owed an explanation said, 'I fell apart when Annie died.' He was quiet for several seconds remembering those days. The awful feeling of loss. Knowing that life would never be the same again. He drank his wine before he continued.

'It was Sabine who saved me from myself. Dragged me, screaming, away from the abyss of turning into a sad and lonely foul-mouthed old man.'

'How did she do that?'

'Locked me in her house and threw away the key.' Johnnie laughed. 'No, she didn't go quite that far but almost. She insisted I moved in with her, cancelled all my delivery work and generally gave me a hard time. Oh, she also had me convert her attic for free while she was at it. Keeping me busy and out of harm's way, she called it.'

'Sisterly love has no bounds,' Rachel said.

'I seriously owe her,' Johnnie said. 'Anyway, it took nearly two years before she decided it was safe enough for normal service to be resumed. I started off with some local deliveries – Dartmouth round to Plymouth, or up the coast to Lymington, across to the Channel Islands, stuff like that – and then we brought Annie over to Roscoff for Martha's birthday. Josette, Carla's mother, was at the party.'

He was silent for several seconds remembering the first time he'd met Josette. How she'd reminded him of a young Annie. How surprised he'd been by the first stirrings of fancying a woman for years.

'We really hit it off that evening and she gave me her number to ring her the next time I was over.' He picked up the wine bottle from the floor of the cockpit and poured them both more wine before continuing.

'That first time she came for dinner on board and I walked her home at midnight. Annie's ghost was still on board then.' He smiled. 'Josette's apartment held no such memories for me.'

'I suppose we saw each other five, maybe six, times in total. As a form of therapy for me it was wonderful that someone liked me enough to sleep with me, but I realised from the beginning it couldn't be a permanent thing. The age gap was too great. So about seventeen months ago I told her it was over.' He sighed before continuing. 'Boy, was my timing out. Apparently I chose to tell her the night she was going to tell me she was pregnant.'

'Would you have continued the relationship if she'd told you?' Rachel asked quietly.

'There's a question,' Johnnie sighed. 'Of course I'd have supported her both financially and emotionally but truthfully? No. I think our relationship had run its course. Josette needed someone younger and now she's met Herve who can give her the life she deserves.'

'Having changed the course of your life irrevocably by handing Carla over to you,' Rachel said.

'There is that,' Johnnie said, holding out his hand for Rachel's empty plate and taking it down to the galley with his own. 'I'll fetch dessert – such as it is.'

When he returned with a packet of millionaire shortbread biscuits, he also brought the official papers Josette had given him.

'Thought I'd see when Carla's birthday is,' he said, opening the envelope and taking out a birth certificate. '5th September. Oh!' He looked at Rachel. 'Her full name is registered as Carla Josette Annie LeRoy.'

'What a lovely gesture from Josette,' Rachel said.

Before Johnnie could say anything, a wave crashed over the bow of the boat, the spray reaching them in the cockpit.

'Time for wet weather gear and battening things down,' Johnnie said. 'We're not going to get much sleep tonight.'

'Going to be a long trip home too, I think,' Rachel said.

Johnnie nodded as he shrugged himself into his waterproof jacket. 'Long and rough. Beating all the way.'

It was twenty-four hours later before they finally sailed alongside the Dartmouth quay after a crossing that had seemed to be never ending. Baby Carla had been awake more than asleep throughout the night, adding her screams to the noise of the wind as Annie battered her way through the waves.

Rachel had done her best to soothe and comfort Carla as Johnnie struggled to keep on course. They were navigating Start Bay before Carla finally fell into a deep sleep and Rachel was able to lay her on the makeshift bed and make them both a much-needed coffee.

Johnnie heard Rachel's muttered 'Home, thank god' and her smothered sigh of relief as the mouth of the Dart hove into view, but made no comment.

As they tied up alongside the quay, Johnnie said, 'You get off home, Rachel, I know you're exhausted. I'll give Sabine a ring and get her to come down and give me a hand with stuff. I need to talk to her anyway.'

'You sure?' Rachel said. 'I'll be off then.' She picked up her kitbag and stepped onto the quay. 'Hope everything goes well with Carla.'

Johnnie nodded. 'Thanks for everything. I owe you.'

Rachel waved a deprecating hand in the air. 'No problem. See you around.'

Chapter Twenty-Four

Sabine

Sabine switched on the kettle in the kiosk before tiredly rubbing her eyes. Another cup of coffee might just jog her body into realising it had to stay awake. Eleven o'clock in the morning and already she was wishing the day was over. Which was wrong on all counts, today of all days. Tonight was her exhibition. She simply had to be fully awake for that.

Life had gone from being busy to being hectic since Carla had arrived in Johnnie's life and in hers by default. Naturally, she was the first port of call for help from her brother – and there had been many calls in the past few days. Not that she minded. She'd adored the little girl from the moment Johnnie had stepped off Annie and handed the baby to her.

'An extra-special present from Brittany,' he'd said wearily. 'Help me get her back to the cottage and I'll tell you everything.'

Sabine had listened intently as he'd told her about his affair with Josette. How he felt morally bound to look after the child while her mother went off to live a life unencumbered.

'How the hell I'm going to cope, I have no idea,' he'd said. 'But once I'd learnt of her existence, there was no way I could walk away.'

Caring for a baby twenty-four hours, seven days a week had never before figured in his life and Sabine knew he was feeling very lost. If he wasn't round at the kiosk or on the doorstep at home, he was on the phone asking for advice. She was doing what she could, of course, but ultimately it still came back to it being Johnnie's responsibility to take care of Carla.

That old cliché, 'steep learning curve', didn't begin to cover the new life experiences Johnnie was going through and if the dark circles under his eyes were anything to go by, it was also currently a sleep-deprived life. Still, he'd always been a quick learner; he'd soon settle into life as a hands-on father.

In the few days since Johnnie had arrived back from France with Carla, her own life routine too had undergone a change. From the moment she'd set eyes on the baby girl, she'd been smitten, remembering how she'd always hoped for a sister for Peter. How quickly she'd agreed all those years ago to Tatty's request to be little Ellie's godmother, the next best thing to having her own little girl she'd decided, only to have her disappear out of her life – until tonight. Tatty had promised to bring Ellie and reintroduce them.

Hopefully Carla would be in Johnnie's and her life for-ever, now they knew of her existence. She did wonder though, how his new daughter would affect his decision to sell the cottage and buy a bigger boat. Probably wouldn't happen now, but Carla was certain to move his life on in a new direction.

One thing she knew for sure, though, the arrival of Carla in their lives meant she could forget any idea of a belated gap year with Owen to far-flung places. No way could she leave her brother to deal with things alone. Not that she'd intended going anyway.

Owen arrived as she made the coffee. Without a word she handed him a cup and poured herself another one. With no tourists on the horizon wanting to buy tickets, they settled themselves in the director's chairs to the side of the kiosk.

'Bliss,' Sabine said. 'Five minutes peace.'

'You all set for this evening?'

Sabine nodded. 'Nervous. And tired. Helping Johnnie with Carla has made me realise just how much my energy levels have diminished as I've got older.'

'Good job you're planning a long holiday at the end of the season then,' Owen said.

'Don't go there, Owen,' Sabine warned. 'Not today. I'm too tired to argue with you. Uh-oh, customers.' And she stood up to greet a couple of middle-aged men who were studying the river trip timetable.

Six hours later, after a half-hour luxurious, reviving soak in the bath, Sabine pulled her long rainbow-coloured velvet evening coat, bought for a snip in one of Torquay's many charity shops, off its hanger and slipped it on. It just added the right degree of 'arty', she felt, over the plain black trousers and long-sleeved T-shirt she'd opted to wear for the opening night of her exhibition.

Her mobile rang. Johnnie. Who else?

'Hi,' she said, picking up her mobile and hoping there wasn't a problem with Carla. No way could she rush round there right now.

'Sabine, I'm really sorry but I might not make it tonight. I can't find a babysitter. Those are words, I might add, that I never thought I'd have occasion to say!'

'Bring Carla with you. She'll probably sleep in her buggy,' Sabine said, stifling a disappointed sigh. 'I really want you there to celebrate with me. If only for ten minutes to hold my hand and have a glass of champagne.'

'I've got one more person to try. If they can't do it, then yes I'll bring Carla. Stop worrying, it's going to be a roaring success with or without me there.'

'I'm not so sure about that,' Sabine said. 'I mean, selling little ink sketches and watercolour souvenirs from the kiosk to gullible tourists is a world away from the contacts Tristan has in the art world.'

'Stop it. Tristan wouldn't have given you this chance if he didn't believe in you. It's his reputation as well as yours that's on show, remember. Now just get down there and enjoy the evening. Hopefully I'll see you later.'

Switching off the phone, Sabine went downstairs.

Peter was in the kitchen ready to walk her down to the gallery. 'Ready?'

Sabine nodded. 'You're looking smart tonight,' she said, registering his new jeans and polo-necked sweatshirt. She kept the thought 'and looking more and more like your dad' to herself. Peter had told her once he could barely remember his father and hated how guilty that made him feel.

'You too. Love your coat. *Très bohème*. Come on then, let's go get your big night started.'

As they walked down towards the gallery, Sabine said, 'I hope people come. Be awful if no-one turns up.'

She knew Tristan had placed an ad in both the Dartmouth Chronicle and the Western Morning News last week and had invited/pressurised some of his contacts into promising to attend. But would they turn up this evening? And if they did, would they like her work? Or dismiss her as an amateur? Was the nostalgia feel Tristan had urged her to go for passé these days?

'Mum. Stop worrying. Of course people will come – if only for the free champagne!' Peter teased.

'Gee, thanks,' Sabine said. 'That really helps.'

The door of the gallery was open and Sabine could see Tristan's sloany receptionist standing by her desk, the usual bored expression on her face. Apart from her and Tristan, the place was empty.

'Sabine, darling, nice and early as instructed,' Tristan said, engulfing her in a hug before handing her and Peter glasses of champagne. 'Here's to you. Excited?'

She nodded. 'More like terrified,' she said as she dutifully clinked glasses with him before taking a nerve-steadying sip and looking around the gallery. Tristan had grouped some nautical paintings together, isolated one or two of the larger ones in a way that somehow seemed to demand the full attention of the viewer. Other smaller ones he'd hung together where they complimented each other.

Even the three more outlandish psychedelic ones Tristan had pulled a face at when she and Owen had carried them in earlier in the week, had been assigned favourable wall space and good lighting. Her favourite one of these had a small red sticker discreetly attached to its frame and she glanced at Tristan, about to ask him who had bought it, but Owen arrived at the moment claiming her attention.

'I can't believe it. Look, that one's sold already,' she said, pointing the red sticker out to him. 'Wonder who bought it so quickly?'

'Me. I bought it last night. Didn't want anyone beating me to it,' Owen said.

'You should have said. I'd have given it to you,' Sabine said, reaching up to give him a thank-you kiss on the cheek.

Owen shook his head. 'I wanted to pay for it. End of. Put the money in the "oldies gap year" fund that you're going to open.'

'Owen, there isn't going to be a gap year fund. Coming on that trip is even more impossible now that Johnnie's got Carla. I have to be here for him.'

'Don't see why. Plenty of people around to help him.'

'They're not family though,' Sabine said.

'True. Anyway, we'll argue about it later. Over dinner. I've booked a late table at the Angel. Thought we'd celebrate in style. Tristan's done you proud,' Owen added, looking around.

'I keep wanting to pinch myself,' Sabine said. 'It all feels a bit surreal to me.'

Over the next ten minutes, the gallery filled up with people and the champagne began to flow. Harriet and Frank arrived and she was caught up in a flurry of air kisses and introductions between Frank and Owen.

'Where's Ellie?' she asked.

Harriet pulled a face. 'I'm really sorry, Beeny, but she's not here. She's had to dash off to Bath. Last-minute commission. She'll be here at the weekend now.'

'Well, at least you're here,' Sabine said. 'Who'd have thought nine months ago when Tristan offered me an exhibition that you, of all people, would be here.'

'Where's Johnnie?' Harriet said. 'Hope he's not away on a delivery. I was hoping to introduce Frank to him.'

'He'll be here later. Trouble finding a babysitter,' Sabine said.

'Excuse me! Since when did Johnnie need a babysitter?'

'Forgot you hadn't heard. Since about a week ago. I'll fill you in with all the details later – or you can ask Johnnie yourself. Here he is now with BB.'

'You made it,' Sabine said, kissing Johnnie's cheek.

'Couldn't not,' Johnnie said, opening his phone. 'Good turnout. Thought I'd take a few mementoes of your first exhibition for when you're famous.'

'I can't believe how many of the paintings have sold,' Sabine said. 'Who's babysitting, by the way?'

'Rachel. I promised I wouldn't be long. So, a few pics, a glass of champagne and I'll be off.'

'When do I get to meet this paragon who is Rachel?' Sabine said. 'Need to thank her for taking care of Carla on the trip back.' Not to mention the fact she was curious to meet this unknown woman who'd become involved in her brother's life.

'I'll arrange supper for one night next week,' Johnnie promised. 'I think the two of you will get on. Now go circulate. Network with the important people.'

Chapter Twenty-Five

Rachel

Carla was already in bed when Rachel arrived in response to Johnnie's last-minute plea for her to babysit for an hour.

'Thanks for this,' Johnnie said. 'I shouldn't be long. Just need to support my sister at her first-ever exhibition. Help yourself to coffee or there's wine in the fridge.'

'No problem,' Rachel said. 'I hadn't anything special planned for this evening.' The fact that she'd promised herself not to get involved with Johnnie or Carla, had seemed irrelevant when Johnnie had phoned sounding desperate. Besides, she'd grown quite fond of Carla in the short time she'd spent with her. Couldn't help wondering how her new life with Johnnie was shaping up.

Once Johnnie had left, quietly closing the front door behind him, Rachel tiptoed upstairs to check on her charge. Carla was fast asleep on her back, one arm tightly clutching the pink rabbit to her chest, a thumb in her mouth. The floor beside the bed was piled with cushions and a folded-up duvet. Johnnie was obviously afraid of Carla falling out of bed. He really needed to buy her a cot, Rachel thought. One of those that converted into a bed at a later date would be ideal.

Leaving Carla to her dreams, Rachel wandered out to the small hallway. Johnnie's bedroom door was open and she peered inside. In contrast to the tidiness he'd displayed on board his boat, the room was a mess. The wardrobe door was open, socks were spilling out of a chest of drawers, the bed unmade. Carla was clearly keeping him busy during the day. Rachel smiled to herself remembering the distant days when Hugo had been a full-time job and she'd been too exhausted to do housework. Johnnie must be on a real roller coaster of experiences right now. Must be doubly hard with no partner to help.

Back downstairs she wandered into the sitting room. After straightening the cream throw on the settee and plumping up the cushions, she picked up some toys and put them in the large cardboard box that appeared to be serving as a toy box before looking at the various pictures Johnnie had on display. Lots of him and a happy, smiling woman who had to be his wife dominated the mantelpiece. A faded picture of a Johnny Onion man and his bicycle stood on a small table alongside a picture of the same man with two young children perched on his knees. Johnnie and his sister Sabine, aged about eight, she'd guess.

The kitchen, when Rachel walked in, was a mess too with the sink piled high with dishes. A quick glance told her there was no dishwasher so, after filling the kettle ready for a cup of coffee, Rachel set to. Twenty minutes later, when the sink was cleared and everything was on the draining board drying, she decided a glass of wine was in order rather than coffee, and went back into the sitting room. Pulling her iPad out of her bag, she settled down to read until Johnnie returned.

He let himself into the cottage quietly just after ten o'clock. 'Good, you've had a glass of wine. Join me in another?' Without waiting for an answer, he fetched the bottle and another glass from the kitchen and poured her one. 'Cheers. Thanks for tidying the kitchen. I don't seem to have conquered the dual art of child-minding and domesticity yet.'

Rachel laughed. 'You will.'

'Carla behave?'

'Not heard a peep from her.'

'Which means I will at approximately one o'clock.' Johnnie sighed. 'Any idea when she'll start sleeping through the night?'

Rachel shrugged. 'Children are all different. I remember Hugo slept through from about a year old but I had friends whose children did it a lot earlier – and some a lot later.' She hesitated. 'You've got to remember too, her mother disappearing from her life and being with you, a stranger, is a major event in her young life. Bound to unsettle her.'

Johnnie nodded. 'A big trauma for everyone.' He glanced at her. 'I realise I'm probably pushing my luck, but can I ask another favour? Will you come shopping with me? Sabine's told me to get myself to the nearest Mothercare and given me a long list of things I need to get.'

'Can't she come with you?'

Johnnie shook his head. 'Too busy working the kiosk at the moment. Please say you'll come. I really have no idea what is good or bad when it comes to things like cots and stair gates, which are top of the list. At least you've been there, done that.'

'A long time ago,' Rachel said. 'It's a different baby world out there these days.'

'So come and help me explore and get to grips with it one day next week, please.'

'Okay,' Rachel said. A couple of hours shopping for things for Carla could be fun. 'Now, how was the exhibition?'

'Good. Lots of people turned up – both locals and some from the art world. Tristan seemed pleased and Sabine couldn't believe the amount of paintings that sold.' He took a swig of his wine. 'So pleased for her. She deserves a break.'

He took his phone out of his pocket. 'I took a couple of photos.' He moved across to sit by Rachel on the settee. 'Mainly of guests rather than the paintings. Here's Sabine hobnobbing with some London critic. 'Here she is with Tristan.'

As Johnnie swiped through the photos, Rachel pointed to one of Sabine laughing with an attractive dark-haired woman.

'Who's that?'

'That's Tatty, sorry, Harriet Lewis. Sabine's best friend from years ago. She's just come back to live in town. Seeing the two of them laughing together is like turning the clock back more years than I care to think about,' Johnnie said. 'I'm hoping she'll agree to be Carla's godmother. Need two, of course,' he paused.

'I was thinking, hoping, that you … I know we don't know each other that well yet, but would you be her second godmother? Seeing the way you are with Carla, I know you'd be a wonderful godmother for her.'

Chapter Twenty-Six

Sabine

Dinner with Owen after the opening night of the exhibition was, Sabine had to admit, rather wonderful. And full of surprises.

The first surprise came as they arrived. Owen was greeted warmly and told his favourite table had been reserved for him. Of all the restaurants in town, she'd never have guessed he was a regular at this particular, expensive, one.

'Favourite table?' she looked at him and mouthed.

'The new chef's a friend,' he shrugged. Besides, you know how much I like French food.'

Sabine nodded, remembering the times in the past she'd cooked Provençal daube or coq au vin for Dave and inevitably Owen had shown up around dinnertime. In the years since Dave's death, she'd invited Owen to share similar dishes with her and Peter more times than she could count.

Sipping a champagne cocktail, waiting for their starters to arrive, she sighed happily. 'I suspect tomorrow will see me brought down to earth with a bump, but I have to say this evening has been one of the best times of my life.'

'No-one deserves it more,' Owen said. 'Is Tristan likely to exhibit your work regularly now, do you think?

He's certainly made a profit on tonight's show, if all the red stickers are anything to go by.'

Sabine smiled happily. 'He did mention something about another exhibition maybe around Christmas time.'

'Did you tell him you'll be travelling then? So maybe a later date would be better,' Owen said, looking at her intently.

Carefully Sabine put her glass down on the table. 'Owen. I'm sorry but, as I keep telling you, there is no way I'm going travelling this year – or any other year come to that. It's just not on.'

'Why not? You've said you'd like to see more places. Mexico. India. America. Might give you some fresh inspiration for your paintings.'

Sabine nodded. 'Possibly, but like many things in my life, I've left it too late. If I go anywhere, it will be a week somewhere in Europe at the most. Nothing that remotely resembles your plans.'

'Trust me, Sabine – it's never too late to change things. Of course, you have to want to.'

Sabine picked up her wine glass and took a sip. 'Please, could we not argue tonight?'

'Sorry,' Owen said. 'Consider the subject changed, but be warned I shall return to it another day. Now …' He paused while the waitress placed their starters in front of them. 'Thanks.'

'I need to talk to Peter soon and tell him what I've arranged with the business. Where and what time would suit you?'

'You want me there?' Sabine said, surprised. 'It's your business. I don't have anything to do with it.'

Owen looked at her. 'Sabine, you know the business wouldn't be the same without your "gift of the gab".'

Sabine laughed. 'Maybe, but it's yours to give to Peter not mine.'

'I want us to do it together,' Owen said. 'So when? Where? Shall I book a table here? Or somewhere else?'

'Why not do it at my place? I can cook something special. Something French.'

'Okay. It's neap tides next week so no evening river trips. Wednesday would be good for me.'

Sabine shook her head. 'No can do. Johnnie's asking this Rachel woman to supper that night for the two of us to meet. No way am I cancelling. I need to meet this superwoman who has arrived in my brother's life. How about Friday?'

'Friday evening it is. Johnnie seems to be revelling in his new role,' Owen said. 'Saw him the other morning happily pushing Carla around town.'

Sabine smiled. 'In typical Johnnie fashion, he's thrown himself completely into doing the single father thing. Reckons he can stay at home until she's two before his savings run out. After that,' she shrugged, 'no idea what he'll do then. Long deliveries will be out, that's for sure.'

'He can always come and skipper one of our boats on a freelance basis if he needs work,' Owen said. 'Next time I see him, I'll let him know the job is there if he wants it anytime.'

Chapter Twenty-Seven

Johnnie

'Who knew places like this even existed?' Johnnie said, looking around him in amazement as he pushed Carla in her buggy into the large baby emporium.

Rachel laughed. 'You're going to need deep, deep pockets this morning. Now, where's the list? We'll start with finding the cot section.'

Two hours later, a mountain of shopping on one side near the cash desk waiting to be paid for, Johnnie was exhausted. Sabine had told him the list contained only essential items. How could one small child need all this?

He glanced at Carla, now sleeping in her buggy after being cooed at and admired by all the assistants during the morning. Her slumped position didn't look very comfortable, Johnnie thought guiltily.

'How long do children stay in pushchairs for?' he said, turning to Rachel.

'A couple of years.'

'Right. I know it's not on the list but let's find her something more comfortable than this buggy then,' Johnnie said.

Fifteen minutes later, a top-of-the-range pushchair had been added to their purchases and they made their way to the cash desk. Johnnie glanced at a box and a pink embroidered dress complete with a matching sunhat Rachel was holding.

'I'm buying her these,' Rachel said. 'All little girls love pink and I think Carla will look lovely in this. I couldn't resist buying her this musical mobile.'

Half an hour later and with his credit card heavily in debt, Johnnie was attempting to fit everything into his car while Rachel held Carla and watched.

'Good job it's an estate,' she said. 'Never have got all this in a normal car.'

Johnnie grunted as he tried to wedge the cot mattress in over the top of everything. Finally he slammed the boot lid down. 'Right, lunch. There's a place down on the front that does great sea food and a glass of wine that has your name on it.'

By the time they'd found somewhere to park and walked the short distance to the restaurant, Carla was awake and grizzly. Rachel watched, amused, as Johnnie quickly found the bottle of milk and jar of baby food he'd placed in the buggy pocket and politely asked the waitress to heat them before they'd even looked at the menu for themselves.

'You're adapting very well to your new role in life,' she said, watching him feed Carla.

'To be honest, I'm feeling overwhelmed by the responsibility,' Johnnie answered quietly. 'She's stopped crying now every time I pick her up so I guess she's getting used to me. But in the middle of the night when she wakes and nothing can soothe her ... then I do worry that I'm out of my depth.' Carefully he tested the temp of the milk on the back of his hand before giving the bottle to Carla to hold.

'*Votre lait pour toi ma chérie*,' he murmured before placing a gentle kiss on Carla's forehead.

'On the other hand, getting down on my knees to tickle and play with her is a sheer delight. I can't believe I have a daughter. I'm terrified of doing the wrong thing. Hurting her because I'm so inept. Sabine has been amazingly patient, answering my child-rearing questions and showing me how to do things, thank god.'

'Children are resilient,' Rachel said. 'Give them lots of love and attention and you won't go far wrong.'

'I might be imagining it, but sometimes I swear she looks at me and then looks around as if wondering who this strange man is and where her mum has gone,' Johnnie said.

'That's something you're going to have to deal with in the future,' Rachel said. 'For now you just have to concentrate on giving her a loving childhood. But if it ever gets on top of you and Sabine isn't around, well, I'm only up the road from you.'

'Thanks. Appreciate it. I already owe you big time,' Johnnie said. 'Can you come to supper Wednesday next week? Meet Sabine. I have a feeling you'll get on.'

'Mmm, not sure about next Wednesday,' Rachel said. 'I've already got a couple of things planned. Maybe leave it for a week or two.'

'Okay,' Johnnie said, smothering his disappointment. 'Let me know when you're free – but please don't leave it too long. Even if Sabine can't make it when you can, I'd still like to have dinner with you.'

What was it with Rachel? Every time he felt they were becoming real friends, she took a step back for no apparent reason and not exactly pushed him away, but it was as if she kept drawing a mental line between the two of them. A line he was finding it impossible to cross.

Chapter Twenty-Eight

Ellie

Ellie dutifully followed the strict instructions Harriet had given her to come via the Higher Ferry. 'It's the only way to come on your first visit. Your first view of Dartmouth will stay with you forever. Shouldn't be too much of a ferry queue on a weekday.'

Ellie knew it was her mum's home town but they'd never visited before and she still didn't understand this sudden waxing lyrical about the place from Harriet and her insistence on having a family holiday there.

The view of the town as Ellie drove round the final bend in the road would certainly stay in her mind – it was far prettier than she'd anticipated. But Mum had got the bit about the ferry queue wrong. There were at least twenty cars in front of her and the ferry was halfway across the river making for the Dartmouth slipway. Why the hell didn't they just build a bridge in this day and age?

Ellie wound her window down, allowing a cool sea breeze to float into the car before settling in for the wait. Forced to sit and do nothing but look at the scenery, she found herself thinking about the way her life after redundancy and the break-up with Rod was working out. These days she rarely thought about him, so that was a good thing, wasn't it? Meant that she was getting on with her life and not wallowing in self-pity like in the early days.

Initially after the break-up, she'd missed her old job more than Rod if she was honest. The lack of a work routine to bury herself in had made the empty days seem even longer. Estelle had been a real saviour there, putting freelance work her way while she pitched ideas to her own contacts. Her work diary these days had several deadline dates for various features she'd been commissioned to write in the next couple of months. She was getting to grips with her novel as well. Writing fiction was so much fun after doing features for all her working life. So things were good really. She was back on track with her working life at least. Plus, Rod was becoming a distant memory.

Cars disembarking off the ferry began to make their way up the hill in a steady stream and as the cars in front of her started their engines and edged their way slowly down towards the ferry, Ellie did the same. One of the last cars to drive on, she was flagged into the right-hand side of the ferry.

Quarter of an hour later, she drove along the embankment, Harriet's instructions on how to get to Swannaton on the dashboard in front of her.

Seeing a parking space on the quay, Ellie pulled in. She had this sudden yearning for an ice cream. Coffee with clotted cream on top. Delicious. Stopping by the boat trip kiosk to finish off the ice cream before it dripped everywhere, she looked at the pictures hanging on the open stable door.

The artist's signature had her taking a closer look. Wasn't that the name of her mother's friend whose exhibition she'd agreed to write a feature on? Mum had said her friend sold her stuff mainly to holidaymakers via her summer job. The woman standing by the kiosk talking to a man with a child in a pushchair, looked about the same age as Mum.

When the woman broke off her conversation to look at her, Ellie said, 'Excuse me, these paintings. Are you the artist Sabine Wills by any chance?'

'Yes.' Sabine smiled at her.

'In that case I owe you an apology. I'm sorry I missed the opening night of your exhibition. I'm Ellie Lewis. Harriet's daughter,' she added by way of explanation.

'Ellie! How lovely to see you,' Sabine said. 'This is Johnnie, my brother, and his little girl, Carla. It's lovely to see you here in town.'

'It looks to be a great place,' Ellie said. 'Can't believe Mum stayed away so long.'

'I expect she had her reasons,' Sabine said, guessing Ellie didn't yet know the truth about Harriet's past. 'Have you been out to the house yet?'

Ellie shook her head. 'No. I'm on my way there now but couldn't resist treating myself to an ice cream. I'd better get going otherwise Mum will be panicking I'm late. Good to meet you both.'

Back in the car and following the one-way route through town and out towards Swannaton, Ellie sang happily to herself, the earlier feeling from the ferry reinforcing itself in her brain. Dartmouth really was a lovely place. It was going to be a good holiday. Life was definitely on the up and up.

Chapter Twenty-Nine

Harriet

Harriet hummed happily to herself as she placed a batch of scones in the Aga. She might be channelling Amy in wanting to welcome people to the house with food, but she felt so good. The sun was shining, the house clean and sparkling. Most importantly, Ellie would be here soon and their family holiday could begin.

But this holiday was more significant than a mere holiday. It was also the week she began her official year of living back in Dartmouth. The week too when she and Frank told Ellie about the legacy and the truth about her own life.

Not knowing how Ellie would react was worrying but, Harriet kept telling herself, Ellie was a grown-up independent woman. She knew the way of the world, that these things happened. Emotionally though, Harriet knew, it was bound to be hard on her.

When Harriet had fully explained why she'd acted the way she had, stressing it had all been done out of love for her and wanting to protect her, Ellie would surely understand and forgive. Wouldn't she? They'd always been so close. Down through the years, avoiding hurting Ellie had always been Harriet's main concern.

At least there was the rest of today to enjoy with Ellie and Frank. No point in diving straight in with the news that was bound to be a shock to Ellie. Let her settle in. A family dinner and then tomorrow 'The Talk' to get things out into the open. Afterwards they could all settle down to a new life back in Dartmouth.

The kitchen door opened and Frank came in from the garden. 'Scones?' He sniffed. 'Smells good. Any chance of one with a cup of tea?'

'Ten minutes,' Harriet said. 'Ellie might be here by then too.'

They were both sitting out on the terrace about to tuck into the scones when Ellie arrived.

'You were right, Mum, Dartmouth is lovely,' she said, giving her a hug. 'Met your friend Sabine by the way when I stopped for an ice cream.'

Harriet's heart skipped a beat. 'You've met Sabine? How was she?' Surely she wouldn't have said anything to Ellie about why they were actually here.

'Nice lady. I apologised for missing her exhibition.' Ellie moved across to Frank and hugged him. 'Hi, Dad. Thought this was a holiday. You look as though you've been gardening.'

'You know me, can't bear to see weed strangling things even in a holiday home,' Frank said lightly, after a quick look at Harriet.

Listening to Ellie chattering away as the three of them sat on the terrace enjoying the cream tea, Harriet began to relax. Everything was going to be all right.

'So freelancing is working out for you,' Frank said.

'Wish in a way I'd started years ago,' Ellie said. 'But then I wouldn't have the contacts I've got now.'

'And Rod?' Harriet asked. 'Have you heard any more from him?'

Ellie shook her head. 'No. All in the past now. He did me a favour, I think, by dumping me. Real wake-up call for me.' She jumped up. 'Right, which room am I in?'

'I've given you one of the rooms with a river view,' Harriet said. 'Come on, let's get your stuff upstairs and I'll show you the rest of the house.'

'While you two girls do that, I'm going to have a shower and then walk into town and pick up some wine for dinner this evening,' Frank said.

'This is a lovely house, Mum,' Ellie said as she followed Harriet up the stairs and into the bedroom. 'Feels more like a private house than a holiday let. How did you find it?'

She moved across to stand by the window before Harriet could answer. 'Wow. Look at the view. All those boats. Any sailing schools around, do you think? Really fancy having a go.'

'I'm sure we can find you somewhere,' Harriet said, grateful that the moment to answer Ellie's question about the house had passed. 'There's an old dinghy hung up in the rafters of the garage. Maybe we'll get that down and I'll teach you the basics.'

Ellie turned to look at her in surprise. 'Didn't know you sailed, Mum.'

'Sailing was always an essential part of growing up here,' Harriet said. 'Sabine and I both had dinghies. I learnt to swim at an early age too.'

She smiled at Ellie. 'Right. I'll leave you to unpack and go and organise dinner. See you downstairs when you're ready.'

Back down in the kitchen, preparing the roast lamb, Harriet felt better than she had for months. She was confident everything was going to be all right. Ellie loved Dartmouth, she liked the house, and she felt they were as close as they had ever been. Pushing cloves of garlic under the lamb skin, Harriet resolved to tell Ellie the truth tonight after dinner rather than wait until tomorrow. Tonight, after a good meal, a glass or two of wine, when they were all feeling mellow, would be better.

Washing the garlic off her hands, she realised she'd forgotten to pick some rosemary from the big bush halfway down the garden. Grabbing the kitchen scissors, she opened the back door to go and get some, at the same time as Ellie walked into the kitchen.

'Back in two ticks,' Harriet said. 'Need rosemary.'

When she arrived back with a big bunch of the herb, planning to hang the surplus to dry with the saucepans hanging on the kitchen-maid rack over the Aga, Ellie was nowhere to be seen.

Peeling the potatoes, Harriet planned how she was going to raise the subject of the past after dinner. After all, she couldn't jump straight into 'so glad you like the house because it will be yours one day' without some sort of lead up. The difficulty would be finding the right words to explain decisions that had been taken in the past.

She glanced up as Ellie came back into the kitchen and froze as she saw what Ellie was holding. Time stood still as she stared at the small silver photo frame Ellie was holding. Where the hell had she found that?

Chapter Thirty

Sabine

'Well, that went well,' Owen said. 'Peter seems happy with everything.'

When Peter had left after supper, impatient to share his good news with his girlfriend, Sabine and Owen had taken their Irish coffees up to the studio. Like she had done so many times in the past, Sabine had kicked off her shoes before curling up on the settee alongside Owen. Relaxing together like the old friends they were. Now though, she stiffened at something in his voice and turned to look at him.

'So he should,' Sabine said. 'You're treating him like the prodigal son, giving him the family business.'

'I've told you before, he's the nearest I'm ever going to get to having a son,' Owen said. 'You and he are my family. Whatever happens in the future.' He placed his drained glass on the coffee table, before catching hold of Sabine's hand.

'Marry me, Sabine. Make us into an official family and me the happiest man in Dartmouth.'

'Oh, Owen,' Sabine said. 'I was beginning to think you'd decided to stop asking me.'

As the silence between them lengthened, Owen let go of her hand, picked his drink up and took several mouthfuls.

'I guess that's a "no" again.' He paused before saying quietly, 'He's not coming back you know. You're wasting your life.'

'Fourteen years after he died, I think I know that. And I haven't wasted my life,' Sabine said, irritated. Maybe the last fourteen years had been lived in the fog of an unrealistic daydream, but she'd still managed to bring Peter up to be a decent person. Surely her mothering skills counted for something?

'Not Dave. Reid.'

Sabine's chest constricted in shock as she looked at Owen.

'You knew about Reid? I never told anyone back then.'

'You didn't have to. Anybody seeing the two of you together could put two and two together and do the maths for themselves.'

'Did Dave?' her voice trailed away.

Own shook his head. 'No – but he never took to Reid either. Called him a smart-ass, as I recall. I'd never have introduced the two of you if I'd known what was going to happen.'

'Nothing happened,' Sabine said quietly. 'I was never unfaithful to Dave.' She fiddled with her glass. 'All these years and you've never mentioned before that you knew. Why not?'

'Guess I was waiting for you to tell me he was the reason you wouldn't marry me after Dave died. Besides, if I didn't acknowledge your feelings for him, I could kid myself I was still in with a chance.'

Sabine hesitated before saying, 'I learnt recently that he's a serial divorcee.'

'You've been in touch?'

'Yes. The night of the party. After I told Harriet and admitted I still had his contact details, she talked me into phoning him. Said it would be a relief to know one way or another. Which I suppose it is.' She ran her fingers through her hair. 'Just damn demoralising at the same time.'

Owen picked up her hand again and held it tightly. 'I'd like to punch his lights out for hurting you.'

Sabine gave a rueful smile. That sounded like a knight in shining armour coming to the rescue.

'It's my own fault for believing happy ever afters existed outside of fairy stories.'

As for failing to realise and embrace the fact that the man sitting next to her holding her hand, had always been prepared to give her the happy ever after she longed for, she deserved the lonely old age she was heading straight for.

Chapter Thirty-One

Harriet

'Mum, have you seen this? The woman in this photo holding a baby looks just like you did years ago.' Ellie held out the silver photo frame for Harriet to look at.

'You've been in Am ... the locked room?' Had she been through the drawers and found the other photos – the ones she'd removed from the sitting room mantelpiece? Carefully she put the potato peeler down and looked at Ellie.

'I was being nosey,' Ellie said, shrugging. 'I saw the key hanging on the hook and wondered if it was to that room. Can't understand why people would lock a room and then leave the key in full view. This was on the desk.' She looked at Harriet. 'You've gone pale.' She glanced down at the photo again before looking up and saying slowly. 'It is you, isn't it? Is the baby me?' She held the photo out to show Harriet.

Harriet briefly glanced at the picture. 'Yes it is me. And ... yes, the baby is you.'

Taken at Ellie's christening, she barely recognised her younger self. How the hell had Ellie? Damn. Having carefully cleared all the shelves in the study of any incriminating photos, she'd left the piles of paper on the desk undisturbed, not realising there was another photo there as well.

'There's something we have to tell you – which Dad and I were planning to do this evening,' Harriet added quickly. 'After dinner.' Where was Frank now when she needed him?

Ellie shook her head. 'Can't wait that long. Come on, Mum, spill the beans about how a photo of us is in an unknown house we've rented.'

Harriet moved across to the dresser where she'd placed an open bottle of red to breathe ready for dinner. 'Pass me two glasses, will you?' she said, indicating the shelf behind Ellie. 'Then sit down.'

Wordlessly, Ellie got the glasses and sat at the table while Harriet poured them both some wine.

'Cheers,' Harriet said before taking a gulp. 'Oh dear, this is difficult. Can we not wait for Dad to be here?'

She took another gulp of wine when Ellie said, 'No.'

'Okay, here goes. To start with, Ellie, this house belonged to Amy, your aunt. We both spent a lot of time here when you were tiny.'

'You've never ever mentioned her before,' Ellie said.

'There's a lot of things I've never mentioned before,' Harriet said quietly. 'Amy died earlier this year. Despite not having been in touch for nearly thirty years, you and I were named as the main benefactors of her will – provided I agreed to a couple of conditions.'

Harriet swirled the wine around her glass and took a drink before saying, 'Which I have. So, this house now belongs to me.'

'What were the conditions?'

'I'm not allowed to sell the house – it has to come to you when I die. That was easy enough to accept. The second clause was harder. I had to agree to live here for a year in order for you to receive a legacy of your own.'

'Why was it so hard to agree to live here? It's your home town. I've never really understood why we didn't come here for visits in the past. And why a legacy for me?'

'Long, sordid story which Amy's will has dragged into the present. Before I tell you, please believe me when I say I've wanted to tell you many times in the past, but for various reasons – fear of upsetting you mainly – I didn't.' Harriet paused before continuing. 'It's your home town too. Aunt Amy was one of your godmothers. The other is Sabine. The thirty-year absence was because I ran away, taking you with me.'

'You left Dad?'

Harriet took a deep breath. 'No, I didn't leave Frank. I left your father.' The words fell into a silence that lengthened for several long seconds before Ellie said, 'Dad isn't ... Dad?'

'He is definitely your dad – both officially in that he adopted you when you were three and because he truly loves you. But no, he isn't your biological father.'

'Who's my real father? Why did you run away?'

'Because your father had an affair,' Harriet said, answering the second question and ignoring the first for the time being.

Ellie spluttered. 'Is that all? You ran away because of that? Why didn't you stay and fight for him? I presume you loved him.'

'It wasn't the same in those days,' Harriet said, wishing Frank would hurry up and return so she didn't have to have this conversation with Ellie on her own.

'It was the town's scandal of the decade. Everyone was talking about the vicar's wife's affair with a parishioner.

And that was before she became pregnant. There was even talk of the church funds being embezzled – thankfully that wasn't true. I left because I couldn't stand being the object of ridicule or pity.'

'She was a vicar's wife?'

Mutely Harriet nodded.

'Was she a friend?'

Harriet shook her head. 'I knew her, of course. We met for the first time in this house but we never really got the chance to be friends. She was only here a couple of months before she stole my husband.'

'What's the name of this woman?'

'Does it matter?'

Ellie nodded. 'Yes, of course it does. I need to know all the details.'

'Vanessa Harford,' Harriet said reluctantly.

'And my father's name?'

'Oscar. Oscar Widdicombe.'

'Do you know where he is now? Can I meet him? I want to know what he's like. I know you think you acted in my best interests concealing things all these years, but I have the right to meet my real father. Which I intend to do.'

Harriet bit her lip as she looked at Ellie. 'I'm sorry, love. He died about a year before Amy.' Her words fell into a silence that lengthened

'You should have told me before. Given me the chance to meet him,' Ellie said. She drained her glass of wine in three large gulps and stood up. 'I'm going out – I need to think. I can't believe this.'

'Dad will be back soon for dinner,' Harriet protested.

'You mean "Frank" will be back. I'm not hungry any-more,' Ellie said. 'I'll see you later.' She was gone, the front door closing noisily behind her.

Frank, returning half an hour later, found Harriet sobbing in the kitchen as she tried to baste the lamb through her tears.

'You've finally told her, then?' he said, taking the roasting tray from her and replacing it in the oven, before taking her in his arms.

Harriet sank against him gratefully. 'Yes, and it's all gone wrong.'

'Where is she?'

Harriet shrugged. 'Went out. Said she wasn't hungry.' She moved out of Frank's arms and reached for a piece of kitchen paper to wipe her eyes.

'Oh, Frank, what have I done? We were having such a good time together before she found a photo of me holding her and started asking questions. I *so* wish you'd been here. I've hurt her so much and I don't know what to do now.'

'When she gets back, we'll sit her down and talk to her together. Explain our reasons for taking the decisions we did. It's all a bit of a shock but I know she'll come round. Angry at first but things will sort. When is her solicitor's appointment?'

'Day after tomorrow,' Harriet said. 'I hadn't even told her about that before she went out.'

Ellie hadn't returned when dinner was ready and Harriet and Frank sat in silence at the table, Harriet literally finding herself unable to swallow the meal she'd prepared. Frank's usual hearty appetite seemed diminished too. Harriet cleared the table, offered Frank another glass of wine before topping up her own glass and said, 'Think I might make a start on Amy's study.'

'Do you want a hand?'

Harriet shook her head. 'Not right now, thanks. I really want to be by myself for a bit.'

In the study she pulled out Amy's office chair and sat facing the computer for several moments before swivelling around and facing the rest of the room. Where to start? So many books. So many files and boxes. What to do with the all the stuff? Who knew whether Amy had any more secrets to be discovered?

Harriet sighed. Maybe it wasn't such a good idea to tackle it on her own. Once Ellie's appointment with Trevor Bagshawe was out of the way, she'd ask both Frank and Ellie to give her a hand sorting it out. Doing it as a family could be a way to help ease Ellie's pain. Talk it all out as they sorted Amy's things.

One thing she could do though, now the secret was out, was to put the photos she'd hidden away out on display again.

Chapter Thirty-Two

Rachel

Sitting in her favourite place, on the top step under the jasmine-covered arch over the three stone steps that led down from the terrace to her small garden, Rachel sniffed the air appreciatively. Early evening and the sweet smell of the night-scented jasmine was heady.

Sipping her glass of rosé, Rachel tried to marshal her chaotic thoughts into some sort of order. To try to make some firm decisions.

The sounds of BB in the kitchen preparing supper for them both drifted out through the open window. Offering BB the spare room had turned out to be one of her better decisions. He was an excellent lodger – more of a friend now than simply a lodger. He'd slotted into the house and her life so well. It was like having Hugo living at home again.

Hugo. Now she had to think about his email that had pinged into her mailbox an hour ago. Suggesting a date for the family to visit. Restlessly Rachel stood up and began to move around the garden, stopping to pull the occasional weed, smell a rose, before leaning against the trunk of the gnarled apple tree that should really be pulled up, all the while trying to sort out things in her mind.

What had Hugo said before she left France? Something about life throwing curved balls into plans. Well, her life had certainly had enough curved balls thrown into it over the years to scupper a national cricket team. The fallout from last year's expected but unhappy event had certainly changed her life. Leaving France was meant to set her on the right course for the rest of her life. She didn't need another of those blasted curved balls winging its way towards her.

One she'd never anticipated. One, if she were truthful, she didn't know how to handle. Running away to avoid the situation that was closing in around her was becoming more and more appealing. But how to explain her reasoning to Hugo? Where to run? Hugo and his family, she knew, would welcome her back to France. Had never wanted her to leave. Or should she go somewhere completely new? Somewhere she could be herself, where the past didn't intrude on the present.

'Another glass of rosé before supper?' BB called from the kitchen.

'Thanks,' Rachel said. She stood up and began to make her way back to the kitchen. 'Something smells good.'

'Chicken with orange and tarragon. My mom's favourite supper dish,' BB said. 'Ready in about fifteen minutes.' He glanced at her. 'You looked deep in thought out there.'

Rachel nodded but didn't explain, saying instead, 'Shall we eat out here? I'll fetch everything.' To her relief BB didn't press her about her thoughts as she covered the table with a cloth and fetched the cutlery.

An hour later, as they finished their meal and Rachel said, 'Truly delicious, BB, thank you,' the doorbell rang.

'Bit late for visitors,' Rachel said.

'Do you want me to go?' BB asked.

'No, it's okay,' Rachel said, standing up as the doorbell peeled urgently again.

Johnnie was standing on the doorstep with a tearful Carla in his arms. As Rachel opened the door, the child leant towards her holding out her arms. Touched, Rachel scooped the child into her own arms and hugged her tight. She sensed Johnnie's relief as Carla's arms went around her neck and she quietened.

'I'm so, so sorry to land on you,' Johnnie said. 'But I'm at my wits' end. I'd have gone to Sabine but she's out tonight.'

'Not a problem,' Rachel said. 'Come on through to the terrace.'

'She's been grumpy all day,' Johnnie said. 'I was hoping once I put her to bed she'd sleep and wake up happier. But if anything, she's got worse.'

He ran his hand through his hair. 'Is she ill? Should I have gone to the doctors?'

Cuddling Carla and gently stroking her head, Rachel looked at Johnnie. 'Her cheeks are very flushed. I think she's teething, poor little mite. You'll need to brace yourself for a long night. Go to the chemist in the morning, they'll suggest something for her gums that will help. In the meantime, if you've any ice cubes at home, try gently rubbing her gums with one.'

'Right. Okay. Will do,' Johnnie said. 'If you're sure that's all it is.' He looked at Carla now sucking her thumb as she snuggled against Rachel. 'Come on then, young lady. Let's get you home.'

Rachel felt the arm around her neck tighten and the child press herself against her.

'How about I walk down to your place?' she said. 'I'm enjoying the cuddle and she's happy for the moment.'

'You sure? She's not too heavy for you?' Johnnie said.

'It's not far. I'll be fine.'

Carla fell asleep as Rachel walked the short distance down to Johnnie's cottage. Rachel gently laid her in the cot while Johnnie covered her with the quilt and they tiptoed out of the room.

Downstairs Johnnie said, 'Do you have to rush? Got time for a glass of wine?'

Rachel shook her head. 'I'd better get back. BB cooked supper so I have a kitchen to clean!' Resolutely she ignored the disappointment on Johnnie's face.

'I should grab some sleep yourself while Carla sleeps,' she said. 'Might be a long night.'

'Good idea,' Johnnie said. 'Rachel, I can't thank you enough for coming to the rescue yet again.'

Before she'd realised his intention, he leant in and kissed her. Not a friendly kiss on the cheek. A proper one on the lips that seemed to Rachel to last forever.

As he moved back, Rachel took a deep breath. Best to stop this before it went any further.

'Let's pretend that didn't happen, shall we?' she said. 'Don't want to spoil a beautiful friendship.'

Quickly she opened the door and left.

Chapter Thirty-Three

Ellie

Ellie had no idea where she was going when she fled the house in Swannaton. All she knew was she had to get away. Find some space to think.

The lights, the sound of disco music from a boat out on the river, the lower ferry ramp clanking onto the slipway, people sitting on the quay eating fish and chips out of polystyrene boxes. All this was lost on Ellie as she pounded along the pavement, determinedly brushing past people enjoying a leisurely stroll in the calm of the evening.

Why the hell had Mum and Da … Frank, kept everything a secret for so long? They should have told her years ago. Slipped it into the conversation when she was, what? Six? Ten? Or even younger. Isn't that what adoptive parents were advised to do these days? Tell the child at a young age? Talk about being the 'chosen' one. Let her grow up with the knowledge. Make it easier to accept. Hell, would they even have told her if this Amy person hadn't pulled the lid off the whole sordid mess with this legacy?

Of course only one half of her had been adopted. Mum was already her mum. Had Frank adopted her because Mum had insisted? Or did he adopt her because he genuinely wanted her as his daughter?

Ellie slowed as she approached the kiosk, remembering how Sabine had chatted to her without the merest hint of having known her as a small child. Had she known that Harriet was about to destroy Ellie's world on this family holiday? So many questions buzzing around in her head.

She sighed. A mere seven hours in this town and again her life had been turned upside down – just when she'd thought she'd got both her personal and working life under control.

Why was she so upset over the news that she was Frank's adopted daughter? She wasn't a child any-more. Or even a teenager with out-of-control hormones reacting to unwelcome news. She was a grown woman who, like Harriet, had been hurt by the actions of a lover in her own life – although, thank god, she hadn't been married to Rod.

Would she have fought for him if she had been or would she still have run and hidden to lick her wounds? Where had she run anyway? Back to Mum and Frank. People whom she knew loved her. People she knew would always take her in. Be there for her, no questions asked. It must have been hard for Mum, leaving Dartmouth all those years ago, with no family of her own to turn to for help.

Ellie stopped in front of the shuttered kiosk, taking some deep breaths and trying to analyse things in a rational way. Was she over-reacting? Thinking about it logically, the news was more upsetting than life threatening. Standing there looking at, but not truly seeing, the river scene, the truth struck her. It wasn't the fact that she'd been denied the chance to meet and know her biological father that really hurt.

It was the knowledge Frank wasn't her real dad that hurt so much. She'd always thought she was more like him than Mum in so many ways. More of his genes had created a special bond between them. Now, the truth was, she didn't share the same genes. The belief had been shattered.

'Are you all right?' A quiet voice broke into her thoughts. 'You're not about to jump into the river, are you?'

Ellie shook her head but didn't turn to look at the woman who'd spoken. If she didn't make eye contact, hopefully the woman would walk on by.

'No is the answer to both your questions. I'm not all right, but I'm not about to drown myself. I've had a shock, but I'll live.'

'Glad to hear it,' the woman said, not moving.

Ellie took a deep breath. She could almost feel the intense gaze of the woman checking her out. Please go away, she willed. If she didn't say anything else, hopefully the woman would get the hint and walk on by. The silence between them lengthened. Finally Ellie sighed and turned to face the woman.

'Honestly, I'm fine. Except … except I'm having a hard time coming to terms with finding out that I'm not who I thought I was.'

'Yes you are. Nobody else can be you. Whatever people say, whatever life throws at you, the only person you can truly be is you.'

Ellie shook her head. 'You have no idea how unhelpful that remark is right now. Thanks for your concern.' She turned away from the woman and began to walk in the direction of Swannaton. She needed to get back to Harriet and Frank. It was time for a no-holds-barred talk. No way was she going to be fobbed off with less than the whole truth from either of them.

Dutifully, Ellie tried to eat some of the dinner Harriet had kept for her before pushing it away. 'Sorry, Mum, nice as it is, I'm not really hungry.' She picked up her glass of red wine and said, 'Shall we do this in Amy's study?' Without a word, both Harriet and Frank followed her.

Ellie stopped as she saw all the photos on the shelves. 'These weren't here before,' she said, walking across to pick one up before turning to look at Harriet.

'I'd hidden them. I wanted to talk to you before you saw them. You finding one I missed, rather pre-empted things,' Harriet shrugged. 'Anyway, I put them back.'

'Is this me being a bridesmaid?' Ellie asked, looking at the photo she was holding.

'Yes. At Sabine's wedding.'

'I've always dreamt of being a bridesmaid – now I find I was one years ago. In another life.'

Carefully, Ellie replaced the photograph on the shelf, glancing at another one of herself in the garden before saying 'Oh!' and picking up another one before looking at Harriet.

'Is this me and my father?'

Harriet nodded. 'Yes.'

'He was quite handsome, wasn't he?' Ellie said. 'How old am I here?'

'The photo was taken on your first birthday,' Harriet said. 'We'd spent most of the day at Paignton Zoo and came to Amy's for your birthday tea. That photo was taken in the garden here.'

'Did I have friends to tea?'

'No. Not that year. It was just the family.'

Ellie sighed as she replaced the photo. 'It's strange, isn't it? You tell me I spent a lot of time in this house as a small child, these pictures show the truth of that, so you'd think

I'd have at least some memories of that time. A sense of déjà vu even, now I'm back. But I don't. Nothing.'

'You were very young when we left,' Harriet said.

Ellie nodded. 'True and I now know why we've never come here as a family before. What I don't understand is, rather than tell me the truth, you consigned your past to the bottom of an abyss and left it to moulder. Why? Did you ever plan on telling me the truth? Were you going to let me find out the truth when you both died? A sentence in the will? Oh, by the way, Frank adopted you and as a family we lived a lie for years.'

'We did what we thought was best,' Harriet said quietly. 'Telling you the truth has always been our intention but, as the years went by, it became more and more difficult. We wanted to give you a secure and loving childhood. Which I think we did.'

'You've deprived me of so much.'

'That's not true,' Harriet protested. 'We were protecting you.'

'I need you to tell me about the kind of life you led here with my father. The things you did together. The places you both took me.'

'Oh, Ellie. Why? That's more my past than yours. You were still a baby. Barely twenty months old when we left. You don't remember any of it. I don't want to go down memory lane in that way. In fact, I won't.' Harriet said. 'It's not fair to me or Dad.'

'Mum's right,' Frank said quietly. 'It's not just you – you're hurting Mum by demanding all this – this superfluous information. We promise we'll tell you everything we can about Oscar and his family. If Mum doesn't want to discuss the life she lived with him, you must respect her wishes. You know the truth now about your birth. Let the rest lie for Mum's sake.'

Ellie was silent before sighing and acknowledging the truth of Frank's words. 'Okay. But I do need to talk about my father. To learn about him. Do I take after him in any way? Do I look like him? What did he do?'

So many questions to ask about the man who, apart from creating her, had had no influence on her life. Would she have been a different person if he'd stayed in her life? She'd never know. If only she could meet him face to face.

'I'm going to try to track down this Vanessa person,' she said decisively. 'If, as you say, she was pregnant when you left, I must have a sibling somewhere in the world. Maybe more than one. They'll be able to tell me what he was like.'

'It's not always a good idea to stir things up by bringing the past into the present,' Frank said. 'You can never tell what the effect will be.' He looked at Ellie. 'Maybe accepting the status quo would be better. You know how much we both love you.'

Ellie moved across to hug him. 'I know you've been a true dad to me and I love you – both of you – to bits, which isn't going to change, but I'm afraid I do have this compelling urge to learn about my biological father even if he was a bastard to Mum all those years ago.'

Chapter Thirty-Four

Harriet

Half an hour before Sabine arrived, Harriet pulled the quiche out of the Aga. A simple green salad was in the olive bowl and a bottle of prosecco was chilling in the fridge. The sun had disappeared over the hills but the evening air was still warm enough to eat supper outside on the small terrace with its view up river.

Frank was away overnight on business so when Sabine had rung and asked could she come out after the evening boat trip had left, Harriet had said, 'Of course. Come for supper.' A girly chat with Sabine was just what she needed to lift her spirits. Since talking to Ellie about the past, all she could think of was how badly she'd handled things. How differently she should have done things. Both now and in the past when all she'd wanted to do was to shield and protect Ellie.

She'd hoped Ellie would join them for supper but that had proved to be a forlorn hope.

'I'll just have a sandwich. I've printed out a copy of Amy's unfinished manuscript and I was hoping to read through it this evening. Then I need to start to do some more research into Vanessa Harford. See if I can find where she is these days. Wouldn't say no to a glass of prosecco though.'

Harriet flinched inwardly at the mention of Vanessa Harford, but said nothing. In one way it was a relief that Ellie was being so open about her need to find the woman; in another way she so wished this search wasn't happening.

She was out on the terrace, placing a couple of late-flowering roses in the centre of the table, when Sabine arrived.

'Lemon cheesecake for dessert,' Sabine said, handing her a cake box.

'Thanks. Sit down and I'll fetch the rest of the food and bubbles.'

'We celebrating something?' Sabine asked as Harriet poured them each a glass.

Harriet shook her head. 'No. I just like it as a summer drink. Santé.'

'Somebody's been busy in the garden,' Sabine said, looking around. 'It's almost back to Amy's standard.'

'Thanks to Frank, really. He's done the heavy stuff and I've done the weeding and replanting.'

'We had some good parties here, didn't we?' Sabine said. 'Nice to think we will again.' She glanced at Harriet. 'You are staying, aren't you? It hasn't been difficult returning, has it?'

'Much easier than I expected,' Harriet said.

'Told you. Most locals have short memories. Besides, these days, people aren't easily scandalised. They accept things with a shrug and move on to their own concerns. Nobody's batted an eyelid at Johnnie suddenly acquiring a daughter.'

'How do you feel about that?'

'I'm an auntie which I adore. I love Carla as much as Johnnie does. Of course there are bound to be problems, especially when Johnnie has to work but we'll manage.'

'He's lucky to have you. It's not easy being a single parent,' Harriet said. 'As both of us know.'

'You talked to Ellie yet?'

'Yes.' Harriet shrugged as Sabine waited for her to say more.

'She's now hell-bent on finding Vanessa and any siblings the woman and Oscar may have provided her with.'

'Only natural she'd be curious.'

'Doesn't stop it hurting though. I admit I was wrong not telling her the truth years ago and I truly regret denying Amy a place in our lives. But what if Ellie discovers another family out there somewhere? One she prefers. Wants to get close to? I don't think I could bear that.'

Sabine reached out and held Harriet's hand. 'I'm sure that isn't going to happen. Ellie knows how much you and Frank love her – she won't dismiss thirty years of happy family life in favour of … in favour of embracing a wicked stepmother.'

'Here's hoping you're right.' Harriet pushed the quiche towards Sabine. 'Help yourself to a slice.'

'I had dinner with Owen the other evening,' Sabine said. 'He asked me to marry him again.'

'This time you said yes?'

Sabine shook her head. 'No. Actually, that's not true. I didn't give him an answer at all. I was too stunned when he told me he's always known about Reid. That I was wasting my life waiting for him to come back.'

'Did you tell him about the phone call?'

'Yes.'

Both women were quiet for a moment, lost in their own thoughts. It was Harriet who broke the silence.

'You should marry him, you know. He's always loved you. He'd never let you down.'

'I know, I know,' Sabine said. 'He's been in my life forever as a friend and I can't imagine a life without him in it. But if I married him and it didn't work, I'd be responsible for hurting one of the best people in my life. I've never wanted to take that risk.' She drained her glass.

'I suppose we're too old to go the "friends with benefits" route?'

Harriet choked on a lettuce leaf. 'Too old? Never. You could always suggest it, but my money is on Owen turning you down. It'll be marriage or nothing with him.'

Sabine sighed. 'Think you're right. He's old-fashioned like that.'

Chapter Thirty-Five

Ellie

Ellie sat back in the office chair, then pushed herself away from the desk and stared out of the window. Eight hundred words written and edited for a feature Estelle had commissioned. A final proofread this afternoon and then she'd press the Send button.

She swivelled the chair so she was facing into the room. At Harriet's suggestion, the study was now regarded as officially hers. Somewhere she could write undisturbed whenever she wanted. She glanced at the three shelves full of Amy's books. So many Cassandra James novels. English, French, Italian, Spanish, Russian editions, along with other languages Ellie didn't recognise, all jostled for space. All written in this room, sitting at this desk.

Would she, Ellie Lewis, ever see a collection of her own books alongside them? Would she be inspired by the simple act of sitting at Amy's desk, using her computer, her chair? Would Amy's spirit linger and offer encouragement? She was probably imagining it, but she did feel different writing in this room.

Since the appointment with the solicitor and the confirmation that Amy had indeed left her a substantial sum of money, Ellie had been struggling to accept how much her life had irrevocably changed and that there was nothing she could do but learn to live with the changes. Whilst part of her fantasised over the freedom the money would give her, a large part of her struggled with the knowledge it came by way of a fragmented family – a family she'd never know.

Harriet tapped on the door before entering carrying two mugs. 'Do you have time for coffee? Or shall I leave you to it?'

'I've got time. I've finished the piece for Estelle and I was sitting here thinking about things – mainly my writing and Amy's books,' Ellie said, taking a coffee. 'Thanks.'

'I wanted to talk about your birthday,' Harriet said. 'How you want to celebrate it. Here? Back home where your friends live?'

'It's weeks away,' Ellie said.

'I know, but depending on what you want and where you want it, I need to at least start thinking about organising it.'

Ellie was silent for a moment. 'How about a small party here? We should still be able to get out into the garden in the evening. If anyone wants to come from Cirencester, we can put them up or they can go to one of the hotels in town.'

'I was hoping you would choose here,' Harriet said. 'It's feeling so much like home to me.'

Ellie picked up Nick Walters' business card, which Harriet had placed on the desk days ago.

'I'm going to ring this agent and see if they'll agree to me finishing Amy's last book.' Thoughtfully she fingered the card before saying, 'It would be a way of me saying thank you to Amy for' —she waved her hand around— 'for all this.' She glanced anxiously at Harriet. 'Do you think that's a good idea?'

'I'm sure Amy would approve,' Harriet said. 'How's the research going for Vanessa? Found where she's hiding herself these days?'

Ellie shook her head. She sensed the unspoken wariness implicit in Harriet's voice. 'No, not yet.' She glanced at Harriet. 'I've found someone who may or may not be connected to her, but I haven't had time to follow it up yet. It's near the top of my to-do list,' she added in case Harriet thought she was cooling off on the idea of finding her father's widow. She wasn't. There were other things she needed to do first.

'Okay. I'll leave you to it. The garden calls,' Harriet said.

Ellie found her mobile and punched in the number from Nick Walters' card. Expecting a receptionist, she was surprised when he answered.

'Nick Walters here. How can I help?'

'Hi, my name is Ellie Lewis and I'd like to talk to you about the unfinished manuscript of my aunt, Cassandra James.'

'I do have a little news about that. We're currently in talks with one of our authors who also writes contemporary women's fiction in the hope she'll finish it for the publishers. I'll be able to tell you more next week.'

'Stop right there,' Ellie said. 'I'm afraid that's not going to happen. I intend to finish it.' Her hand clutching the phone suddenly felt clammy.

'Are you a writer?' Nick asked.

'Yes. Well, more of a journalist – but I am writing my first novel.'

'I think the publishers would prefer a well-known novelist to finish the book.'

'Amy left me the rights to all her books,' Ellie said. 'Which I take to include the unfinished one. You only get it to sell it if I can finish it. Otherwise,' she took a deep breath. 'I shall finish it and either find another agent or self-publish.'

There was a short pause before Nick said, 'I think we'd better have a face-to-face chat. Are you in London? Can you come to the office before the weekend?'

'I'm in Devon at the moment. Not sure I can get to London for a couple of weeks,' Ellie said, not adding that she was already planning to spend every available moment working on Amy's manuscript.

'I'll come down and we'll discuss it,' Nick said. 'I'm off on holiday to Portugal at the weekend for a couple of weeks so it will have to be when I get back. Just promise me one thing? Don't talk to any other agent or publisher in the meantime.'

Chapter Thirty-Six

BB

The cryptic message Johnnie left on Rachel's answer phone for him was intriguing.

'Eleven o'clock by the kiosk this morning if you can. Might have some boat info.'

Several people were crowded around the kiosk booking tickets for the next river trip, when BB walked along the quay. Johnnie, crouching down and pointing out things on the river to Carla in her pushchair, stood up when he saw BB.

'Glad you could make it,' Johnnie said. 'You free for the next hour or two?'

'Sure am. You found me a boat?'

'Possibly. Forty-footer, name of Chevalier. Moored up at Stoke Gabriel. Once Sabine is free, I'll hand Carla over to her and we'll go take a look.'

Half an hour later, they were in Annie's tender and motoring up river. Passing Annie herself on her mooring in the middle of the river, BB said, 'Don't suppose you're thinking of selling her, are you? She pretty much ticks all my boxes.'

'I was thinking of selling, but things have changed now I've got Carla,' Johnnie said. 'I'm going to sell the cottage and buy a bigger place but keep the boat.'

'Tell me about this Chevalier then,' BB said.

'Built locally at Uphams, Brixham, late 1940s. She's forty foot with a beam of nearly ten foot and recently been refurbished. Had several good sails on her. Belongs to a friend who's going through a messy divorce. Looking for a quick sale.'

As they passed Dittisham, Johnnie pointed to a motor launch tied to the end of one of the mooring trots. 'There's a famous boat for you.'

'Looks like it could do with a paint job,' BB said.

'It's one of the Dunkirk little ships,' Johnnie said. 'Everything on her is in its original condition. Played a huge part in getting men back from France. Not what you're looking for, but it's also up for sale.'

BB took a long look at the launch as they passed it, shaking his head. 'Amazing what they achieved. So much history.'

Johnnie slowed the outboard motor as they approached Stoke Gabriel. 'There's Chevalier. Middle of that line.'

'Can we get on board?' BB asked.

Johnnie nodded. 'Key's in my pocket. Like the look of her, then?'

'Sure do.'

Johnnie cut the outboard as he took the tender alongside Chevalier and BB tied a painter rope to the yacht's rail before stepping on board and waiting in the cockpit for Johnnie to join him and unlock the hatch.

He didn't say anything as he stepped down the four steep steps into the saloon and explored the yacht. The galley had the usual sink, gimballed cooker, small fridge and compact storage space. The chart table, easily accessible from the cockpit was opposite and the main saloon with its table and red leather bunk seats was inviting. A double cabin, shower and the heads were built into the remaining forward space with the sail locker in its usual place in the bow.

'Great refurbishment,' BB said as he joined Johnnie in the cockpit. 'Old wooden boats always seem to have a soul, like a living thing. There's something cosy about a teak-lined boat cabin.' He glanced at Johnnie.

'Sorry, a bit sentimental there but ...' he shrugged.

'So, what do you think?'

'You said you'd sailed on her? How does she handle?'

'Good. Came a respectable third in a race at last year's Regatta,' Johnnie said, closing the hatch and locking it. 'I can arrange a sail for you later in the week, if you're interested.'

'Thanks. I'm more than interested. I think you've found me my ideal boat,' BB said. 'I owe you one if it all works out.'

With Johnnie at the tiller of the tender as they moved away from Chevalier and began to motor down river, BB smiled as he looked back at the yacht. 'She's got lovely lines,' he said. He turned to look at Johnnie.

'Nobody else after her, is there? I'm not likely to be gazumped? Willing to put some money on the table to reserve her.'

'Ian, the owner, was going to register her with the agencies this week. Once he knows how serious you are, I'll get him to hang fire until you've had a sail and shaken hands on the deal. Okay?'

'Thanks.'

They were almost back down at the kiosk when Johnnie said, 'Is Rachel okay?'

'She seems fine,' BB answered absently, his thoughts still on board Chevalier. 'Why do you ask?'

'Haven't seen her around for several days. She was supposed to be getting back to me over something, but I haven't heard a word.'

'Want me to mention you're waiting to hear from her?'

Johnnie shook his head. 'No worries. I guess she'll be in touch soon. If not, I'll pop round and see her.'

Chapter Thirty-Seven

Rachel

Rachel glanced at the bedside clock. 5.30 a.m. Exactly five minutes since she'd last looked. She sighed. After tossing and turning for most of the night, she might as well accept the fact that she was unlikely to get any more sleep. Far better to dress and go for a walk. Try to let the fresh air clear her mind.

Dressing quickly and pulling on her jeans and sweatshirt, she crept downstairs. No shower. She didn't want to disturb BB. Quietly she opened the front door and let herself out.

Passing Johnnie's cottage on the way into town, she wondered how he was coping with Carla's teething. She hadn't heard from him for some days now – not since the night she'd fled, panic-stricken, from his cottage. Carla's teething pain had probably been helped by a visit to the chemist, but she hadn't liked to tell Johnnie the problem would be there for months yet.

Deserted streets felt strangely alien as Rachel walked quickly through Fairfax Place and onto Newcomen Road. She could sense the town stirring – the strident noise of an alarm clock coming from an open window, the smell of brewing coffee floating past, bundles of newspapers left in front of the closed newsagent's door waiting to be sorted – but met no-one as she walked out of town. The absence of people served to reinforce her current sense of once again being an outcast.

Turning at Warfleet and walking in the direction of the castle, the jumble of questions in her mind had combined to form just two. To leave? Or to stay and to hell with the consequences? Decisions! Decisions!

St Petrox church, perched on its rock at the head of the river, beckoned as Rachel stood and looked out to sea. She hesitated before walking towards it and pushing open the gate and entering the churchyard. Rose petals from a recent wedding littered the path. A typical ancient cemetery unfolded as she wandered around.

Humps in the grass where graves had lost their headstones. Ancient memorial stones at a crazy angle. Lichen-covered grave stones. Fallen slabs, their carved letters battered by the elements out here on the cliff undecipherable.

A headstone where she could just make out the inscription, 'Beatrice. Beloved daughter. 25 May 1895– 20 February 1896', had her wiping a tear away. Eight months. Younger than Carla was now.

Carla. Should she accept Johnnie's offer and become the child's godmother? So much of her wanted to say yes. Longed to be in her and Johnnie's lives. She could treat Carla as the daughter she'd never had. Accepting though would mean becoming involved. Being truthful about the past.

Rachel bent down and picked a daisy growing on the child's grass-covered grave. To stay – one petal pulled. To go – another petal pulled. She liked Johnnie and that kiss had confirmed what she'd suspected. He liked her too. Wanted more. Moving the tentative friendship they'd formed onto a different footing – a full-blown relationship – wasn't possible. Was it?

More petals pulled in the daisy game she'd not played since childhood – yes to stay, no to go, yes, no, yes. She should never have returned. Far better to leave the past undisturbed. Return to her life in France with Hugo and family.

The daisy had five petals left. No, yes, no, yes … no. Rachel's lungs hurt as she let a deep sigh go.

Closing the churchyard gate behind her, Rachel began to make her way back to Dartmouth. She'd have a holiday somewhere and put the house on the market when she returned. Hugo could visit as planned and then she'd leave – go back with him to France. Decision made. Time to move on. Now to start the process of leaving.

Chapter Thirty-Eight

BB

BB took his breakfast coffee and toast out to the terrace and sat enjoying the quiet early morning silence. A silence occasionally broken by squawking seagulls and the distant sound of cars driving onto the Higher Ferry car ramp drifting towards him on the breeze.

Between eating his toast and drinking his coffee, he studied the bus timetable he'd picked up yesterday and began to plan his day out. A ride out to Torcross to look at the Sherman tank, lunch in a beachside restaurant and then back on a bus to go to Kingsbridge for the afternoon.

A shiver of anticipation ran through him as he thought about what he hoped to discover later that day. If he'd read his most recent genealogy research correctly, in a few hours he could have the confirmation of the existence of 'The English Connection' that he and Jessie had set out to find. Or not.

A deep sigh escaped his lips as he folded the timetable back up. He prayed placing so much hope on this one Kingsbridge name and address didn't lead to a dead end and disappointment.

'That was a deep sigh,' Rachel said, making him jump in surprise. 'Good morning.' Holding a mug of coffee, she sat down in the chair opposite him.

'Good morning,' BB said, concealing his surprise at seeing her. He'd realised the first morning after moving into the cottage that Rachel was most definitely not a morning person, and he'd taken great care not to disturb her in the mornings.

'You're up and about early,' he said.

'Couldn't sleep, so I went for a walk,' Rachel said, looking at the bus timetable. 'Where are you off to then?'

'Torcross and Kingsbridge.'

'More family research?'

BB nodded. 'Yep.'

Rachel warmed her hands around her mug of coffee before asking, 'You are happy here aren't you, BB? The room's worked out okay? You're staying until September?'

'Couldn't be happier,' BB said. 'Why? You're not about to give me notice, are you?'

Rachel shook her head. 'No. It's just … I thought I'd go away for a bit and wanted to make sure you'd still be around to keep an eye on the place.'

'Sure thing. You planning on going on another yacht delivery with Johnnie, then?'

'No. Thought I'd have a holiday. Go down to Cornwall or somewhere. No idea where yet really – or when. Just feel the need for a change.'

'Happy to look after the place any time – so long as you're back before September,' BB said. 'I was going to ask you this later, can I invite a few friends around for drinks on the terrace sometime?'

'How many is a few? Not a lot of room really,' Rachel said.

'About seven or eight. You too, of course, if you haven't disappeared on holiday by then,' BB looked at Rachel hopefully.

'Don't see a problem with that number. Okay.'

'Thanks. Right. Quick shower and then time to get going. I'll see you this evening, with some good news I hope.'

For BB the slowness of the bus journey from Dartmouth along the coast road to Torcross was just perfect. He admired the blue sea and the golden curve of Blackpool Sands bay as the bus climbed the hill towards Strete, then through Strete where he held his breath as the driver jiggled the bus through a seemingly impossible narrow space to pass a Dartmouth-bound coach.

He was given a quick glimpse of the long stretch of Slapton Sands with its sea sparkling in the sunlight in the distance as the bus drove along the final stretch before the final descent. Minutes later, the driver drove slowly down the hill, round the last bend and into Strete Gate at the start of the long, straight drive into Torcross itself, with only the wide shingle beach between it and the English Channel.

Getting off the bus in the centre of the village, BB crossed the road and made his way to the Sherman tank memorial. Standing to one side, he waited patiently for the crowd surrounding the tank to disperse and allow him to approach for a better look. A pile of paperback books was stacked neatly on a table near the tank and he picked up one.

The Forgotten Dead by Ken Small. He'd briefly looked through this book in the reference library the other day. Now he could buy his own copy and read it properly. He knew it detailed the tragic events that had happened out in the bay in front of him the night of April 27 1944. The night that Great-uncle Lance, one of the men involved in the naval exercise – code name Operation Tiger – had died. Hard to reconcile the dreadful events of that night with the peaceful scene before him now.

Listening to the man at the tank telling the story of how after forty years the tank was dragged from the bottom of Start Bay and placed here as a memorial to all the young men who died that night, BB felt increasingly sad for his late great-uncle. No wonder Grandfather had never talked much about his time here.

The book bought and safely placed in the folder with his research notes, BB made his way across the road and walked along the beach for a while. His head needed the sea breeze to blow away all the harrowing pictures his mind had conjured up listening to the tragic outcome of Operation Tiger and how it had affected the whole coastline.

Two hours later, his head cleared by the sea air, and fortified by some of the most delicious fish and chips he'd ever eaten, he was back on a bus for the last stage of his journey to Kingsbridge. He knew from the map he'd printed off the Internet that the street he wanted was at the top end of the town's steep main street.

Reaching the top of town and following his map, he found the address with surprising ease. He stood in front of the terraced cottage, its front garden a mass of flowers and its white-painted wooden garden gate firmly closed, for several moments. He was excited about the answers he was hoping to get. But what if he was wrong wanting to bring this family and their past into his life? What if they weren't interested in having overseas cousins? Would they resent him appearing out of the blue and disrupting their lives? If they told him to get lost, then he would. Tell Jessie that there was no English connection, but he had to know one way or the other. He took a deep breath and put his hand out to lift the gate latch.

'If you're selling something, we're not interested. We're not interested in being saved either. So please don't waste your time – or ours!' A woman about his own age stood on the doorstep of the cottage.

'No, I'm not doing either of those things,' BB said, opening his file and taking out a photocopy. 'I'm looking for somebody.'

'You're American?'

BB nodded. 'I'm afraid so. May I?' And he opened the gate and walked up the path. 'Do you recognise this lady?' He handed her the photocopy of Lance and Florrie. Saw her start as she looked at the picture.

'That's my grandmother,' she said, looking up at him and handing back the paper.

'So your mother must be Mrs Elisabett James?'

When the woman said a simple 'yes' and nodded her head, BB wanted to punch the air. 'Is your mother still alive? Does she live here? Can I meet her?'

'Who are you?'

'I'm Braxton Brael – always called BB – and I think we may be related.'

'You'd better come in,' the woman said. 'Mother's in the back garden. I'm Patricia, by the way.'

Expecting to find Elisabett James simply sitting in the garden enjoying the sunshine, BB smiled when he saw her bending over, vigorously weeding a flower border. Like his own mother, she clearly refused to give in to age.

'Mum, this is BB from America. He'd like to talk to you about Grandma Florrie,' Patricia called out.

BB watched as Elisabett straightened up, a hand placed in the small of her back, and turned to face him.

'It's a pleasure to meet you, ma'am,' BB said, striding forward, hand outstretched.

Elisabett shook his hand but didn't respond. Her blue eyes, regarding him from behind rimless glasses, gave nothing away as she waited for him to continue.

'I've been researching my family history and I think we're related.'

'Now what makes you think that, young man?' Elisabett said in her soft Devonshire accent.

BB handed her the photo. 'The man in the photo was my Great-uncle Lance and I understand the lady was your mother.' Watching her as she looked at the picture, BB saw her hand tremble and tears glisten in her eyes.

'I'm sorry, it must be a shock for you,' he said, looking across at Patricia, who was also watching her mother.

'Mum, why don't you and BB sit on the patio and I'll go make us all some tea?'

Once she'd settled herself on one of the cushioned teak chairs, Elisabett glanced at BB. 'This is the first time I've ever seen a photo of my father. Mother didn't have one. He was a handsome man, wasn't he?' She looked at BB. 'I can see the family likeness.'

'Jessica, my sister, is sending the original over. When it arrives, it's yours,' BB said. 'There's also some letters Florrie wrote to him on the days they couldn't meet.'

'She was never told officially, you know, that he'd died,' Elisabett said. 'The official channels of information were all denied to her because they weren't married or related. It was only when news of the tragedy started to circulate in town that she knew something dreadful had happened to him.'

'That must have been so hard for her,' BB said quietly.

Elisabett nodded. 'It was. She rarely talked about the war or him when I was growing up, although my stepfather never let me forget I was not his.'

Elisabett took off her glasses and wiped her eyes with the back of her hand. 'It wasn't until I was a teenage rebel that I demanded to know everything about him and announced that I was off to find my American family that she finally opened up about him.' Elisabett shook her head.

'She had very little to tell me really, except she was heartbroken when he died. Said he was the love of her life.' Fiddling with her wedding ring, she continued, 'She never even had the chance to tell him about me. Didn't have an American address for the family either. All she knew was that he came from somewhere in South Carolina.' Elisabett laughed. 'Imagine if I'd carried out my threat and gone looking – it would have been like trying to find a sprat in a shoal of mackerel.

'I, of course, have spent many years dreaming of my American family arriving on the doorstep and whisking me away, and now you've finally turned up.'

Patricia arrived just then with a tray laden with tea and scones.

'You all right, Mum?'

Elisabett nodded, blinking back the tears.

BB took her hand in his. 'Did your mother know Lance's brother Randy, my grandfather, was a GI too?'

'She never said. Did he die in the tragedy too?'

'No. He wasn't on board the boats that night. If my grandparents had known about Lance and you, I know they would have made every attempt possible to contact your mother.'

'Nobody knew about them,' Elisabett said. 'That was one thing mother did say. The locals weren't really allowed to mix with the army. Security was tight – although not tight enough, it seems. Their love had to remain a secret from everyone until after the war was over.'

She took the tissue Patricia handed her and wiped her eyes.

'So how did you find me?'

'Serendipity,' BB said honestly. 'Randy met a Dartmouth girl too, Mary Seale – maybe your mother knew her? Their love had a happier ending, even though Mary's family disowned her. Mary ran away to America and they were married in 1946. Jessica – that's my sister – and I have been researching, trying to find the Seale relatives. Who, incidentally, appear to have died out. I just happened to see the record of your christening with Lance named as your father.' He took the cup of tea Patricia passed to him. 'Thanks.

'I couldn't believe it, to be honest. I haven't told Jessica yet about you. I wanted to make sure it was true before I said anything. I only wish Grandpa Randy and Grandma Mary were still alive. My mother though, will be thrilled.'

'That was something else I missed out on – loving grandparents. My mother's parents never got over the scandal,' Elisabett said. 'After mother married, she and my stepfather moved to Brixham and simply lost touch with her family. Probably still got relatives over there in Dartmouth too that I know nothing about.'

She picked up the plate of scones that Patricia had placed on the table in front of them and offered it to BB, along with a bowl of clotted cream and jar of homemade jam.

'Dysfunctional families existed long before the twenty-first century,' she said, laughing as he helped himself to a scone. 'I'm so happy part of mine is finally – how would you phrase it? Ah, I know, getting it together.'

Chapter Thirty-Nine

Sabine

Sabine sat in one of the director's chairs outside the kiosk and fanned herself with the Dartmouth Chronicle she was too hot to read. Just gone three p.m., and the heat was intense. She didn't dare look at the thermometer pinned to the kiosk wall. The last time she'd looked it had said twenty-seven degrees and that had been hours ago. It felt hotter than ever now, the gentle breeze coming off the river doing little to cool things down.

The town was quiet with very few people wandering around. Families had gone to the beach, day-trippers had taken refuge in various cafes and sensible locals were staying indoors until things started to cool down. The trip tonight, due to set off at seven o'clock, was only half full but Sabine anticipated a last-minute rush of bookings as the heat died and people visualised the enjoyment of spending a couple of hours out on the water in the cool of the evening.

Looking out across the river to where Owen's boats were moored, she caught the occasional glimpse of Owen and Peter on board Queen of the River, doing some routine maintenance. Since he'd learnt about inheriting the business, Peter had taken over more and more responsibility for the day-to-day running of the business, even telling Owen they needed to talk as he had lots of plans for expansion next season, much to Owen's amusement.

She smiled as she saw Johnnie walking towards her, clutching ice creams in one hand and struggling to push Carla in her pushchair with the other.

'You're a star,' she said, accepting the coffee-flavoured ice cream cone with its 99 chocolate flake. 'Just what I needed. I was too lazy to walk up and buy one.'

For several minutes they concentrated on eating their ice creams before the sun melted them. Johnnie, though, fought a losing battle with Carla's face and hands as her chocolate ice cream dripped faster than she could lick it.

'Owen talked to you recently about the trip?' Johnny asked as he searched in the pushchair bag for a wet wipe to give Carla's face a clean.

'You mean apart from constantly nagging me to go with him?'

'He's planning to go to Thailand now, you know,' Johnnie said. 'He's made contact with a woman over there.'

Sabine stared at him.

'Maybe he'll come back with a mail-order bride,' Johnnie said, not looking at her.

'Over my dead body!' The words were out before she realised the significance of them. How jealous she felt at the suggestion.

'See, you do care. Don't worry, I made that up to see your reaction.' Johnnie looked at her.

'Seriously, Sis, why the hell don't you a) go travelling with him and b) marry him.'

'Travelling with him would mean leaving you to cope with Carla without any backup,' Sabine said, ignoring the second question.

'Not a good-enough excuse,' Johnnie said. 'Carla and I are settling in together just fine. Besides, I do have women friends in town, you know. Harriet and Rachel, to mention but two.'

'Ah, Rachel. You deliberately keeping her away from me?' Sabine said, glad of an opportunity to steer the conversation away from her and Owen. 'If she knows I'm your sister, I'm surprised she hasn't come by the kiosk and introduced herself.' She looked suspiciously at Johnnie. 'She does know I'm your sister?'

Johnnie nodded. 'Of course. She was busy the evening I suggested supper and now she's away for a couple of weeks. When she gets back I'll introduce you. Promise.'

'Make sure you do.'

'So,' Johnnie said. 'No worries about me not coping with Carla while you're away. And then, when you get back, Carla will love being a bridesmaid at her Auntie Sabine's wedding. Won't you, *ma chérie*?' He looked at Carla, smiling.

'Hey, slow down,' Sabine said. 'Agreeing to go travelling with Owen is one thing. Getting married is maybe a step too far.'

'It's a step you should have taken years ago,' Johnnie said. 'Right, we're off to the park.'

Sabine bent down and kissed Carla. 'Have fun. See you soon.'

Johnnie was so much happier these days since Carla had appeared in his life. It was because he finally had a purpose again, Sabine decided. She couldn't help wondering though whether it was just Carla who'd put a spring in his step, or whether this Rachel had something to do with it as well. She must make a real effort to meet and become friends with her.

Folding up one of the chairs to put away, the Save the Kiosk poster she'd pinned to the door at the beginning of the season caught her eye. Faded by the sun, the writing was illegible and she reached up and took it down. No point in leaving it up there.

The petition itself was languishing on the shelf by the biscuit tin. Guiltily Sabine realised she hadn't accosted anyone to sign the petition for weeks now. Thoughts about the kiosk had slid to the back of her mind recently. She doubted too that Johnnie had given it any thought since the arrival of Carla in his life.

Sabine turned to deal with a couple of holidaymakers who wanted to book tickets for a boat trip at the weekend. By the time she'd issued their tickets and entered the details on the boat's booking form, Owen was standing at her side waiting for her to be free.

'Seen BB recently?' he asked.

Sabine shook her head. 'No. Why?'

'Remember the boat Chevalier? Used to belong to old Harry the river pilot years ago. BB's buying it.'

'Good for him.'

'He's planning to sail it back to America, September/October time,' Owen said. 'Looking for crew already. Reckons he only needs two.'

Sabine looked at him, already knowing what he was going to suggest but waiting for him to say it.

'I've agreed to be one of his crew. You up for being the other one? You said you wanted to see America. Perfect opportunity.'

Sabine bit her lip, Johnnie's earlier comments still resounding in her thoughts. Was this crunch time? Did she want to commit herself to this right now? If she agreed, there would be no backing out. She'd be letting BB down as well as Owen if she changed her mind.

She took a deep breath. 'Bit rusty as far as sailing goes. I haven't done any for years.'

'It's not something you forget how to do,' Owen said. 'Besides, you can always become the galley slave.'

'Chauvinist,' Sabine said. 'Okay. I'll do it. We'll go see the world together.'

She placed a subtle emphasis on the word 'together' and hoped from the look on his face that Owen had heard and picked up on the unspoken message in the reply she had just given him.

LATE SEASON

Chapter Forty

BB

Out on the garden terrace, BB switched on his laptop and opened the video calling feature. If he'd timed it right, both Mom and Jessica would be home. It was Jessica who opened the connection.

'Hi, Bro. What's up?'

'Nothing. Everything is great. Really great,' BB said. 'Is Mom there? I've got news to share.'

He waited while Jessica shouted 'Mom. Golden boy wants to talk to you!'

'Do wish you wouldn't call me that,' BB said. 'It's so not true.' He checked his video was up and running. He wanted to see both their faces when he told them the news.

'Hi, Mom. How you doing?' he asked as she appeared next to Jessica.

'Fine. So what's this news?' Marilyn Brael said.

'I've found the perfect boat,' BB said, failing to fight his urge to tease Jessica, knowing how much she wanted an English connection. 'It's a beautiful wooden ketch. Everything I wanted in a boat.'

'Pleased for you,' Jessica asked. 'Is that it?'

'Yes. No.' He paused. 'I've also found and met the English connection.'

'Woah!' Jessica said. 'We really do have relatives over there? Seale or Holdsworth? How closely related?'

'Neither. Connections to both those families appear to have died out. But we do have cousins here for sure. I've met with them.'

'If the link has died out, how come?' Jessica asked.

'Great-uncle Lance.'

'Impossible. He died in the war,' his mother said.

'Like Grandpa Randy, he met and fell in love with a local girl,' BB said. 'She was pregnant with a baby girl when he was killed. He never knew, so couldn't have told Grandpa who would, I know, have done his darnedest to find her and help.'

'So is our great-aunt over there still alive?' Jessica said.

'She's dead but her daughter, Elisabett James, is very much alive. She has a family too. Elisabett is two years older than you, Mom. Her daughter, Cousin Patricia, is in her forties and so is her brother Oliver. Haven't met him yet. He lives somewhere called Cumbria.'

'Did you take photos when you met them?' Marilyn asked.

'I forgot. Too excited. I'm seeing them again soon. Will take some and email them to you.'

'Make sure you do. Tell them any time they want to visit, they'll be more than welcome.'

'They've already issued the same invitation to you,' BB said. 'So hopefully you'll all get to meet soon. I'm here for another couple of weeks if you want to come over?'

Marilyn shook her head. 'Too much going on here for the next month. We'll arrange a visit for next year. Now, tell us about the boat you've found.'

For the next five minutes, BB talked about Chevalier, filling them in on its history and saying how much he was looking forward to sailing her back to Southern Carolina.

Fifteen minutes later, he cut the Skype link having been caught up to date by Marilyn and Jessica with things going on back home and sat back, a smile on his face. Marilyn and Jessica were already talking about a holiday in England next year and he was definitely going to hold them to that. He wanted them to meet Rachel too.

With Rachel away on holiday, he'd got into the habit of spending more time in the cottage, enjoying the freedom of having time on his own in such delightful surroundings. It was like a second home to him now. The day Johnnie had introduced him to Rachel had been a fortuitous one for him.

Briefly he wondered if Johnnie had managed to contact Rachel before she went away. Somehow he doubted it. She'd been in a hurry to go. Said something about a lucky cancellation in the hotel of her choice somewhere down in Cornwall. Hopefully she was having a good time, he'd thought she'd looked rather strained before she left.

Before he closed the laptop down, BB checked his emails. Johnnie had arranged for him to crew on Chevalier tomorrow in one of the Regatta races and he lived in fear of it being cancelled. No email to that effect, so an early start in the morning. He couldn't wait.

Chapter Forty-One

Harriet

A perfect early evening during Regatta Week and the Lewis family were together on the terrace, each enjoying the moment in their own way.

Harriet, looking out across the river to Kingswear, remembered long-ago years when she'd stood here waiting for the Red Arrows to show off their aerobatics. Frank, his binoculars trained on the yachts returning from racing out in the bay, thought about learning to sail, while Ellie was curled up in one of the ancient cane chairs flicking through a glossy magazine.

Earlier they'd been in town soaking up the atmosphere of Regatta Week and watching the dinghies sailing on the river. Harriet couldn't get over the number of activities that were available all week.

The town bustled with life from early morning to late at night. The river, chock-full with boats of all sizes including two tall ships and a naval frigate, was a sight to see, particularly at night when many of the yachts were dressed overall. Harriet couldn't remember it ever being so crowded.

'Regatta's grown so much. We always had the funfair, the slippery pole, crabbing competitions and fireworks, but now there is so much more. As for the street entertainment, it's amazing.'

'Think I might take up sailing,' Frank said, the binoculars now fixed on one particular yacht making its way up river. 'Looks more exhilarating than golf.'

'That reminds me. I need to organise getting the old dinghy in the garage checked out so I can teach Ellie to sail,' Harriet said. 'Want me to teach you, too?'

'Not dinghy sailing,' Frank said. 'I fancy something bigger. Like that one.' And he pointed to the sleek thirty footer he'd been concentrating on.

'Mmm,' Harriet said. 'Moorings are hard to come by these days. They'll have to be quick to pick up their moorings,' she continued. 'I think all movement on the river is forbidden while the Red Arrows are doing their display.'

'How long before they start?' Ellie asked.

'About quarter of an hour,' Harriet said, glancing at her watch. 'Feels strange being out here with just the three of us waiting. Amy issued an open house invite every year to watch the Red Arrows. This terrace and the garden were always crowded with her friends. Next year I'll organise a BBQ.'

Hearing her mobile phone inside on the kitchen table give a short ring indicating she had a message, she said, 'I'll fetch the jug of Pimms from the fridge and see who that was.'

Harriet read the message from BB and quickly texted a reply before going back out to the terrace. She paused in the doorway, taking in the scene before her. Her heart had always belonged to Dartmouth, to this house even, and right now life was just about perfect.

Ellie was pointing out something to Frank in the magazine she'd been reading and they were both laughing.

The two of them had always shared the same sense of humour and could cry with laughter over something that Harriet found only mildly amusing. Both great practical jokers, Harriet had learnt early on to be very alert on 1st April, or suffer the consequences. Inevitably, one or the other of them always managed to fool her.

She was so lucky to have met and married Frank. He'd adored Ellie from the beginning. As far as he was concerned, she was his daughter. End of. Nothing had changed for him when she'd announced she needed to find the woman who was effectively her stepmother and learn about Oscar.

'I wish she didn't feel the need to do it, but I do understand,' he'd said. 'I'm just glad I don't have to compete with him in person. If he were still alive, I might feel different.'

Struggling with tears Harriet had hugged him. 'Love you.'

Standing there watching her favourite two people in the world, Harriet sent a silent 'Thank you' skywards. Amy had been right to force her to return and live here.

Ellie's determination to track Vanessa Harford down was difficult to accept, but subconsciously Harriet knew fighting her on the issue was pointless. It was something Ellie had to do, leaving her with no choice but to accept and support.

'BB has invited us for drinks at seven o'clock on Sunday evening. Wants to celebrate and say thank you to all his new friends for a great summer,' Harriet said, moving out onto the patio with the drinks.

'Me too?' Ellie said. 'I don't really know him.'

'Of course you're invited as well,' Harriet said. 'Next week we must start organising your birthday do. The 5th of September will be here before we know it.'

'Listen,' Frank said. 'I can hear planes out at sea.'

Seconds later, the nine low-flying small red aircraft of the Red Arrows screamed past them in formation, going up river, and the display started.

Both Ellie and Harriet had their hands over their ears in a futile effort to lessen the incredible sound. The sky was soon riddled with red, white and blue vapour trails as everyone held their breath watching the planes performing a tightly choreographed dance in the sky together before moving apart and doing separate tantalising manoeuvres. One last dip of the wings and they were gone, disappearing seawards as quickly as they arrived.

'Wow,' Ellie said. 'That's left me on a high – goodness knows how the pilots feel. Should think their adrenaline is off the scale for weeks after a performance like that. At one time I thought two of them were going to clip the tall ships masts, they were flying so low.' She shook her head. 'Wow. And wow again.'

Chapter Forty-Two

BB

With an hour to go before his party, BB mentally checked his list, hoping he'd not forgotten anything. Champagne and wine in the fridge – tick. Beer and red wine on the terrace table with glasses – tick. Nibbles consisting of large packets of crisps and tortillas – tick. Cheese and biscuits – tick. Mini pasties – tick. Florentine biscuits to go with the coffee he planned to offer before everyone left – tick.

He hoped everyone he'd invited would come. So many new friends he'd made over the summer months but, having promised Rachel it wouldn't be a large crowd, he'd tried to keep the guest list small. He guessed there'd never be more than eight or nine of them on the terrace at any given moment during the evening.

Johnnie had phoned to say he'd pop in early while Sabine babysat Carla before going home to let Sabine come. Harriet had said she, Frank and Ellie were looking forward to it. To his delight, Elisabett and Patricia had promised to drive over from Kingsbridge for the evening. BB smiled to himself. Introducing his English relatives to his friends promised to be the crowning event to an exciting few days.

Regatta Week had been amazing. The atmosphere in town, the thrill of crewing on board Chevalier in a race where she was placed second overall but first in her class had confirmed she was the boat for him.

Everything was now going ahead for him to buy her. Just a week or two whilst Johnnie helped him sort out the formalities – and he transferred the dollars – and she'd be his.

A knock on the open front door and Johnnie called out, 'Hello?'

'Come on through,' BB shouted.

'First to arrive, am I?' Johnnie said. 'Haven't yet got used to planning my social life around the demands of Carla.'

'No worries. We can have a glass of champagne together before everyone arrives. It gives me time to thank you personally for everything this summer.'

As BB poured the drinks, Johnnie noticed a picture postcard of the Scilly Isles propped up on the mantelpiece of the sitting room.

'Rachel?' he asked, indicating the card.

'Yeah. She's having a great time down on St Mary's.'

'Any idea when she's due back?'

BB shook his head. 'Not a clue. Ah, Harriet, Frank and Ellie are here. Let's party.'

Elisabett and Patricia were the next to arrive, followed within minutes by Owen. BB made the introductions with a happy smile on his face.

'Meet my newly discovered English relatives,' he said. 'I can't tell you how happy I am to say that. My Dartmouth summer has been just perfect,' he continued. 'I've found the English Connection and, thanks to Johnnie,' he raised his glass in Johnnie's direction, 'I've bought a boat. Mission accomplished.'

Johnnie raised his glass. 'Cheers to that. Time for me to go home now and for Sabine to party. Bye, everyone. Thanks, BB.'

'Bye,' Harriet said absently, looking across the terrace to where Ellie and Patricia were talking together and helping themselves to nibbles. She turned to Frank.

'Am I imagining it? Do you think there is a certain likeness between those two? I mean I know Patricia is a bit older but ... ' Her voice trailed away as she continued looking. 'They look so similar to me.'

'Mmm, they've both got the same shaped faces and neither of them are tall,' Frank said. 'They've both got brown hair too. Maybe that's what makes them appear alike.'

'No, it's more than that,' Harriet said. 'I wonder how their connection to BB came about.'

'Why don't you ask BB or Elisabett if you're interested,' Frank said.

'I'm probably imagining things that aren't there but I will later. Oh good. Sabine's here.'

Once Sabine had a glass of champagne in hand, BB took the three of them across to introduce them to Elisabett and Patricia, who was still talking to Ellie.

'So pleased you found some relatives,' Sabine said. 'Is it a connection to the Holdsworth family like you were hoping?'

BB laughed. 'You remember our first conversation. No not the Holdsworths. A much more recent connection than that through my Great-uncle Lance.'

'How come?' Sabine asked.

'Operation Overlord down on Slapton beach. He and my granddad were GIs and Uncle Lance met the love of his love before he was killed. One Florrie Widdicombe, the mother of Elisabett.'

'My father is a Widdicombe,' Ellie said, unable to contain herself. 'I wonder if we're related.'

Elisabett looked at Frank. 'I thought your name was Lewis. You certainly don't look like a Widdicombe.'

'That's because I'm not,' Frank said.

'No, I meant my biological father,' Ellie said quickly. 'He was somebody called Oscar Widdicombe. He's dead now. Maybe we're related too?'

'Told you,' Harriet muttered to Frank. 'Not just round faces.'

'I can see more research coming up for everyone,' Sabine said.

'Not necessarily,' Harriet said. She took a deep breath as everyone looked at her.

'When Oscar and I were planning our wedding, I discovered his grandfather had a sister who had been cut off from the family because of an affair during the war. Her name was Florence Widdicombe. Apparently she was always called Florrie. Oscar and Amy never met her.'

Everybody looked at Harriet in stunned silence for several seconds, before the noise of the front door slamming closed made them all jump.

'Hi, BB. I've come back early especially for your party. Hope there's still some champagne left,' and Rachel walked out onto the terrace to join them.

Harriet stared in disbelief at the woman and clutched at Frank's arm as the words 'Vanessa Harford' escaped unbidden from her lips and she fainted.

Chapter Forty-Three

Harriet/Sabine

The next morning, as Harriet stacked her breakfast things in the dishwasher and Frank drank his second cup of coffee, Ellie wandered into the kitchen and said, 'I'm going to visit Vanessa this morning.'

'Of course you are. Why wouldn't you?' Harriet said, slamming the lid of the dishwasher closed. 'Now the woman's living on our doorstep. Makes it easier for you.'

'Mum! It's something I need to do.'

Harriet sighed. 'I know it is, but that doesn't make it any easier.'

Ellie walked over to her and gave her a hug. 'I want to talk to BB too. I could be another long-lost cousin of his.'

'I'd almost forgotten BB's news. Vanessa's appearance overshadowed everything else for me,' Harriet said. 'Don't think there is any doubt there is a family connection with BB. American cousins could be fun.'

'I'll see you later then,' Ellie said. 'Probably treat myself to lunch in town. Ciao.'

Harriet methodically dusted crumbs off the table before asking Frank, 'You got any plans for this morning?'

'Gardening. Unless you want to do something?'

'Thought I'd go and talk to Sabine.'

When Harriet approached the kiosk later that morning she found Sabine and Johnnie shouting at each other in French. Neither of them noticed her and she stood back, remembering their fiery arguments in the old days. Best not to get involved. It was only when she saw Sabine throw up her hands in a typically Gallic manner and Johnnie storm off, that she ventured to get closer.

'Dare I ask what that was all about? Looked a bit heated,' she said.

'Just told him about Vanessa turning up and he went all pious on me,' Sabine said. 'Said it didn't matter to him.'

'Well, why should it?'

Sabine sighed and began to tick points off her fingers. 'Because, one, Rachel Mansell stroke Vanessa Harford is the woman who sailed with him to France when he came back with Carla. Two, she's the woman who went baby shopping with him. Three, she's the woman he turns to for emergency help if I'm not around. Four, I know he really likes her and five, he's just told me he wants her to be—' Sabine stopped. 'Oh my God. Sorry.'

'What?' Harriet said.

'He's asked her to be Carla's Godmother – with you.'

Harriet closed her eyes for a couple of seconds and sighed. Vanessa Harford was back, once again threatening to disrupt her life.

'Are you all right?' Sabine said. 'No after effects from falling?'

Harriet opened her eyes and shrugged. 'Got a bit of a bruise on my thigh. Otherwise I'm fine. What happened last night after Frank and Ellie took me home?'

'Not much. Vanessa vanished upstairs when you fainted and everybody left soon after you.'

'I still can't believe she's been here in town all summer,' Harriet said. 'How come Johnnie didn't recognise her?'

'He'd never met her before. You remember in those days he was often away crewing for months. Think he was on a research ship somewhere in Antarctica when Oscar fell for her charms.'

'She must have realised you were his sister.'

'Think she's spent the summer avoiding me, to be honest,' Sabine said. 'She knows, like you, I'd have recognised her instantly.'

'I remember you both meeting at Aunt Amy's party,' Harriet said. 'You clicked with each other immediately.'

'We did but we fell out pretty spectacularly over you and Oscar. We almost came to fisticuffs in the street. I never spoke to her again. They left soon after, and now she's back,' Sabine said. 'Any ideas on how we handle things?'

'Absolutely none,' Harriet said, shaking her head. 'I also have the added complication of Ellie. Personally, I could kill Vanessa for the past, and yet part of me can't help thinking if she hadn't run off with Oscar, I wouldn't be so happy and married to Frank. And Ellie wouldn't have had such a wonderful childhood.'

'Johnnie really likes her too, so the pressure is going to be on me to be friends with her,' Sabine said.

'Meantime, Ellie is at this very moment making her acquaintance,' Harriet said. 'She's desperate to learn about Oscar.'

A family group approached the kiosk and Sabine turned to give them her attention. Harriet waited patiently while Sabine issued tickets and made genial conversation with them.

As they moved away Harriet said, 'I know Frank is finding it easier to accept this 'need to know my real father' attitude that Ellie has adopted because Oscar is dead and there is no chance of them coming face to face. Or having to share Ellie's affection.'

'Whereas Vanessa is very much alive, in town and back in your life,' Sabine said.

'Exactly. Am I going to be forced to stand by and watch the woman who irrevocably changed the course of my life become friends with her stepdaughter – my daughter? I dread the thought of bumping into her around town,' Harriet shuddered. 'Four months into the year of living here to comply with Aunt Amy's bequest and this happens. Eight long months before I can return to my own home.'

'Don't let her drive you away a second time,' Sabine said. 'Johnnie told me to leave the past where it belongs, in the past. He wants me to meet her soon.' She paused. 'I'm thinking of going to see her before he arranges anything. See what she has to say all these years later. Want to come with me?'

Harriet shook her head. 'No. I need a few more days to calm down. Have to say, it's beginning to look like it's a case of forgive and forget for you at least.'

Sabine pulled a face. 'I have to try for Johnnie's sake – and I think you know you have to do the same for you and Ellie.'

Chapter Forty-Four

Ellie

Ellie slowed her pace as she walked up Clarence Hill. Arriving hot and flustered on Vanessa's doorstep was not part of the plan. Not that she'd formulated much of a plan beyond arriving on Vanessa's doorstep – or should she start thinking of her as Rachel?

BB was coming out of the house when Ellie reached it.

'Hi. Not sure how newly discovered cousins umpteen times removed should greet each other,' BB said. 'But I'm sure it's in order for a peck on the cheek,' he said, as he leant forward and kissed her.

'Morning, Cousin,' Ellie said. 'You got time to talk?'

'Not right this minute. I'm late to sign the papers for my boat. Dinner this evening? Eight o'clock at The Royal?'

'Look forward to it,' Ellie said. 'Is Rachel in?'

BB nodded and pushed the door open. 'Rachel, you've got a visitor. Go easy on her,' he whispered. 'She's a bit fragile this morning. You'll find her out on the terrace.'

The sitting room was tidy as she walked through. In the kitchen the dishwasher was whirring away but the work surface was still littered with the debris of last night's party as Ellie walked out to the terrace.

Rachel looked at her and indicated she should sit in the chair next to her. Then she offered her a coffee from the cafetière on the table.

'Thanks,' Ellie said.

'I thought you or your mother would turn up,' Rachel said. 'How is Harriet? Not too many bruises from last night?'

'She seems fine. Thanks for asking. I'm curious – why were you expecting her to come?'

'To take the opportunity of telling me to my face how much she hates me?'

'Mum wouldn't do that. She doesn't like confrontation. Besides, I don't think she hates you – just dislikes you for what you did. There is a difference,' Ellie said.

'And you're here because?'

'To learn about my father obviously.'

When Rachel didn't answer, Ellie said, 'By the way, your remark the other evening – "whatever people say, whatever life throws at you, the only person you can truly be is you" when you thought I was about to jump into the Dart, wasn't helpful.'

'That was you?'

Ellie nodded. 'I'd just learnt about you. Ironic, really, you should be the one to be concerned about me.'

'People do what they do. Few people can claim to live a life without regrets along the way. I know I can't,' Rachel said. 'In the end, it has to boil down to being true to yourself.'

'Do you regret stealing my father from my mother and me?'

'I regret that people got hurt when Oscar and I fell in love, but I've never regretted loving Oscar.' Rachel stood up. 'I need something to eat. Toast?'

Ellie shook her head. 'No thanks.' She followed Rachel into the kitchen and waited while she cut bread for the toaster and placed plates, cutlery, butter and marmalade on a tray.

'Mum says you were pregnant when you left. Do I have a brother or a sister?'

'A brother. Hugo.'

'Shame. I was rather hoping for a sister,' Ellie said. 'Does he know about me?'

'No. We never found it necessary to tell him.'

'A mistake you've made in common with Mum then. You should tell him. You never know, we might meet one day and fall madly in love and want to get married, then where would we all be?'

'He's married.'

'That didn't stop you and my father. I'm not married. Toast's burning.'

Rachel sighed. 'I like burnt toast.' She picked up the tray and went back out to the terrace. 'You want to be married?' she asked, setting the tray down on the table.

'I expected to be married and have a family by now,' Ellie said. 'I live in hope of meeting Mr Right one day.' She sighed. 'Sooner rather than later, if possible. Anyway, back to my father.'

Rachel buttered a slice of toast and took a bite.

'So what is it you want to know about Oscar?'

'Everything you can tell me. What he liked, what he did, any little traits of his I might have inherited.' She paused. 'Whether he felt any guilt about losing contact with me – or whether he didn't care.'

'Oh, he cared all right,' Rachel said. 'I don't think he ever got over not seeing you grow up. He did wonder if you'd seek him out when you were older, but he was determined you had to be the one to make contact. He felt Harriet had suffered enough without him appearing back to disrupt her new life demanding to see you.'

'Do you have some photos? I've seen one of Oscar holding me on my first birthday, that's all. I'd love to see what he looked like in later years.'

'I have a few. I'll fetch them.' And Rachel stood up to go indoors.

Ellie, waiting for her return, remembered another question she needed to ask.

Rachel returned carrying a small photo album which she placed on the table in front of Ellie.

'There you are.'

'I've just realised I don't know what to call you,' Ellie said. 'Technically I suppose you're my stepmum but I'm a bit too old to regard you as that. So, do I call you Vanessa or Rachel?'

'Rachel.'

'Okay.' Ellie opened the album and began to turn the pages. 'Oh, that's a lovely photo. You look very happy.'

'We were,' Rachel said. 'That was taken on our twentieth wedding anniversary in Antibes.'

'He still looks like he did in the one of us together years ago.' Ellie flicked through to almost the back page before saying, 'Although in this one he looks older. Where was this? He looks different in this one.'

'Switzerland. Two years ago,' Rachel said, her voice breaking.

Ellie glanced at her and realised how tearful she was looking. 'I'm sorry. This must be even harder for you than me. You'd known and loved him all those years and now he's gone. I've only just learnt about him so can't miss him.'

'A year ago I couldn't look at these without breaking down, so I guess that means I'm adjusting to life without him,' Rachel said, closing the album.

'So where do we go from here?' Ellie said.

Rachel shrugged. 'I'm leaving soon. I'd already decided to return to France before anybody discovered who I was. I just wish I hadn't come home early for BB's party. If I hadn't, nobody would have been any the wiser. It was a major mistake on my part to come back.'

'I was already looking for you on the Internet,' Ellie said. 'Wouldn't have been long before I found you anyway.'

'Google has a lot to answer for,' Rachel said.

'Can I visit you in France? Meet my brother?'

Rachel looked at her for several seconds before nodding her head. 'You'll have to give me time to tell Hugo about you – but yes, you can visit.'

'Thank you,' Ellie said. 'I'd better go. Thanks for talking to me. Can we meet again before you leave so you can tell me more?'

'We'll have lunch one day before I leave,' Rachel said. 'Ellie, you have the same confident air about you that Oscar always had. I think you probably inherited his stubborn streak too.'

Chapter Forty-Five

Rachel

Half an hour after Ellie left, Rachel went for a much-needed walk to try to clear her head. The moment Harriet had fainted at the sight of her last night, her mind had started buzzing with what the consequences might be. She was thankful that it was Ellie, not Harriet, who'd arrived at the house this morning. Ellie's visit, demanding information about Oscar was the first – and quite possibly the simplest – consequence to deal with. Talking to Harriet would have been a lot harder.

Not that talking to Ellie had exactly been easy. Showing her the photos had raised so many memories, some she'd rather forget. Seeing the Switzerland photo had brought so much emotion flooding back into her body. It was going to be even harder the next time they met. Ellie seemed determined to ask her to dig deep into her memories and tell her things about Oscar that should stay buried with him.

Four days after Regatta and the town was quieter as Rachel made her way through, but there were still holidaymakers around. Dodging around a group of meandering sightseers, she stopped outside one of the several estate agencies in town and took a deep breath. Autumn was probably not the best time to try to sell the house, but she needed to get things moving. Resolutely she opened the door and went in.

'I'd like to make an appointment for someone to come and value my house and put it on the market,' she told the woman on the desk. 'ASAP,' she added.

The woman made a note of the address, took her telephone number, checked the diary and suggested, 'Four o'clock tomorrow? Fine. Mark will see you then.'

Stepping back out into the street, she found Johnnie and Carla were waiting for her. Ah, the second consequence of last night's party. Johnnie wanting an explanation.

'Saw you earlier but you'd disappeared in there before I could catch you,' he said with a jerk of his head towards the estate agency. 'We need to talk,' he continued. 'Carla needs a nap so coffee at my place?'

Tiredly Rachel nodded. No point in putting it off.

Johnnie led the way through town and Rachel followed as best she could, the narrow pavements and people window-shopping making it impossible for her to walk alongside him and the pushchair.

Back at his cottage, Johnnie quickly made Carla a drink before taking her upstairs and settling her down for her nap. Downstairs, Rachel filled the kettle, flicked the switch and waited.

Johnnie, when he returned, busied himself with spooning coffee into mugs before looking at her.

'According to my sister you're that notorious woman, Vanessa Harford, who stole Harriet's husband many moons ago.'

'That just about sums it up,' Rachel said. 'Think notorious is a bit harsh though. It wasn't something I set out to do.'

'Returning under a false name all these years later though had to be a deliberate decision,' Johnnie said. 'Why?'

Rachel ran her hand through her hair and took a deep breath. It was important to tell Johnnie the truth.

'To get closure on my life with Oscar. To be able to move on with honesty. After he died, I found myself thinking more and more about the way our life together had started out here. The way we'd hurt people – and never said sorry.'

'Why return under a false name? That wasn't honest.'

'I know,' Rachel sighed. 'I needed to come back here to draw the final line under my past life. But at the same time, I didn't want to have people pointing the finger at me, remembering my thirty-year-old ...' She hesitated. 'Crime is the wrong word, although I suspect that is how people viewed it back then.'

'I'm told Harriet felt much the same. In her case she was afraid of being pitied and becoming, as she saw it, a laughing stock again,' Johnny said, pouring boiling water into the mugs.

Rachel looked at him. 'I'm truly sorry she felt like that. Personally I was relieved to find the town full of incomers. The people I'd known had moved on – with the exception of your sister – and, of course, Harriet.'

Johnnie handed her a mug and leant against the work surface.

'Did you know Sabine and I had the most spectacular row down by the kiosk after Oscar and I got together?' Rachel said. 'As Harriet's best friend, I think she felt it was her moral duty to tackle me about it. She, almost literally, tore me to shreds over the affair.'

Johnnie shook his head. 'No, she's never mentioned it. I guess Sabine was the reason you sidestepped all my attempts to introduce the two of you over supper? You knew she'd recognise and expose your secret.'

Rachel nodded. 'I couldn't risk it. She was, and is, unlikely to lay out the welcome mat for me. Especially now that Harriet is back living in town.'

There was a short silence before Johnnie spoke. 'I told Sabine this morning how I feel about you.'

Rachel sipped her coffee. 'Exactly how do you feel about me?'

'I was beginning to feel that Rachel Mansell could be someone special in my life. Daring to hope that she might like me too.' Johnnie put his coffee mug down and folded his arms against his chest before saying quietly, 'You're the only woman apart from Annie that I've ever felt like this about. But now I'm told you're not who I thought you were. Hell, I don't even know what to call you now.'

'How about sticking with Rachel? I was christened Vanessa Rachel so it is my name. I think I prefer it to Vanessa, to be honest. I'm still the same woman who's enjoyed the time we've spent together.' It was important that she told him that.

'Are you serious about selling the house and leaving?' Johnnie asked.

Rachel nodded. 'Yes. Instead of getting the closure I wanted, I've opened up everything again so it's better to leave. Minimise the damage.'

'You could stay and face things. No?' This as Rachel shook her head. 'Where are you going? Back to France?'

'Back to my family.'

'If I were to ask you to stay, see if we could get through this together and see if we had a future together, would you?'

Rachel hesitated. 'Not sure Sabine or Harriet would like that.'

Johnnie glared at her and swore in French before saying, 'I don't give a damn whether they like it or not. It's me who's asking you to stay.'

Rachel closed her eyes and took a deep breath, weighing up her words. She liked Johnnie more than she'd admitted even to her inner self. Could she live in the same town as Harriet and Sabine? Would it make life difficult for them having her around? Would they make life difficult for her? Opening her eyes, she looked at Johnnie.

'Their presence, particularly Sabine's, in your life, makes it difficult for me to stay. I'd hate to come between you and your sister.'

Johnnie moved across to her and took hold of her hands. 'Your regrets are pointless without action. Talk to Sabine. Talk to Harriet. Get real closure and begin again. With me.'

Rachel tried to pull her hands away. 'I must go.'

Johnnie tightened his grip. 'Please at least promise me you'll think about it. It's ridiculous allowing a thirty-year-old feeling of guilt to rule your present and the future. The world has moved on for all of us.' He leant in and placed a gentle kiss on her forehead before freeing her hands.

Rachel turned away from him and left.

Walking the short distance home from Johnnie's, she began to weigh up her options. Lie low for the next few months until the house sold and she could leave. She could do that. The consequence of that particular action though would mean giving up any chance of a future with Johnnie. A future that she acknowledged inwardly would be a good one, filled with a growing love and a future she was beginning to visualise and desire.

If, on the other hand, she did as Johnnie suggested and talked to Harriet and Sabine, it might be possible to stay in town. Would they even want to see her, let alone talk to her? But if she didn't try, she'd never know the answer.

There was still the unanswered invitation to be Carla's godmother to deal with as well. Impossible to accept when her real identity was a secret. Equally impossible to accept and stand alongside Harriet in church without the two of them burying the past.

Reaching her front door and pushing the key into the lock, it struck Rachel how limited her choices were. The personal closure she'd come back to town to find for herself had proved elusive. Instead she was being urged to give others the chance to be involved in the closure. Her reward? A whole new life with Johnnie.

She just had to find the necessary courage to do as he suggested. Talk to Harriet, sort things between them and, hopefully, have her belated apology accepted. Then they could both move forward.

Today she couldn't summon up enough strength to deal with any more emotion, but maybe tomorrow she'd walk out to Swannaton and finally apologise to Harriet for stealing her husband all those years ago.

She'd leave meeting with Sabine for another day. Maybe one when she had Johnnie at her side.

Chapter Forty-Six

Harriet

Harriet stood back and surveyed the pine kitchen table. Normally covered with a cloth, she'd spent the last twenty minutes vigorously cleaning it, having decided she'd prefer to use it uncovered.

The repetitive scrubbing of the wood had proved to be therapeutic. She'd worked a lot of angst out of her system, leaving her feeling calmer than when she'd started the job. Not that she was totally calm. However much she wished it was otherwise, the problem was still there and had to be dealt with. She couldn't avoid it for much longer. Especially since last night at supper when Frank had thrown his suggestion into the mix.

'I think we should relocate here permanently,' he'd said, helping himself to another spoonful of the ratatouille she'd made to accompany the family supper of lamb and couscous.

'You want to sell the Cirencester house?' Harriet said. 'Our home for the last twenty-five years.'

'This feels like home now,' Frank said. 'If we sell and invest the money, I could even retire early.'

'I agree with Dad,' Ellie said. 'Sell up and enjoy life here. If you do though, you'll have to agree to let me move back home permanently. I love it here.'

Harriet had looked at them both. How could she say she'd felt the same way too since the beginning of summer, but now, knowing Vanessa was back in town made her feel like running away – again.

'We'll have a family conference at the end of my obligatory year of living here, and then decide,' she said, ending the discussion. By then things should be clearer in her mind. Conversation had petered out at that point.

'Table looks good,' Ellie said, wandering into the kitchen in search of coffee. She switched the coffee machine on.

'Thanks,' Harriet said. 'We need to talk about your party. How many of your old friends are likely to come?'

'About ten, I think, the others are all busy,' Ellie said. 'I'd like Rachel to come too, but I know you won't want that. It's okay to invite BB though, isn't it?'

'BB is fine,' Harriet said, ignoring the mention of Rachel.

'You should go and see her, you know,' Ellie said. 'I like her. I think you would too if you gave her a chance.'

Harriet stiffened. 'Bully for you,' she said. 'I don't want to talk to her, or about her.'

'She says she's going back to France once the house is sold. Says I can visit and meet my half-brother.' Ellie poured herself a coffee before saying, 'Right, I'm off to do some more work on Amy's book.'

Alone in the kitchen, Harriet poured herself a coffee and took it out to the garden to drink. Leaning against the trunk of the old apple tree like she had done so many times in the past, she sipped her coffee and watched the Lower Ferry making its way across to Kingswear.

This unexpected reopening of the thirty-year-old Vanessa affair could, if she insisted on harbouring old grudges, spoil the life she had now. After all these years did the fact that Oscar had left her for another woman matter? In truth, she'd got over it years ago.

She was married to a man she loved and was happy. These days she barely knew anyone of her generation who hadn't been divorced at least once. What had made headline news all those years ago, barely registered in people's consciences these days.

Ellie, as a result of being told the truth about her father, had a whole new life opening up for her. There was this half-brother in France she was already planning to meet. BB and his family in America would no doubt also welcome her. Nearer home there were the Kingsbridge cousins. Ellie would soon find herself as part of an extended international family that wouldn't include her parents – unless she, Harriet, put the past behind her conclusively.

Sabine had already urged her to talk to Vanessa and now Ellie was encouraging her to do the same. So why not just do it? If Vanessa refused to see her, she could at least tell Ellie she'd tried.

Resolutely Harriet finished her coffee and returned to the house. Now was as good a time as any. Grabbing a jacket from its hook in the hall and throwing it over her shoulders, she opened the front door and came face to face with, 'Vanessa!' she said involuntarily. 'This is a surprise.'

'I'm Rachel these days. Can we talk please?'

Harriet stood aside. 'Come in.' She led the way into the small sitting room and closed the door.

'Sorry if I caught you on your way out but I won't keep you long,' Rachel said. 'I realise it's thirty years too late, but I want to say sorry for the hurt Oscar and I caused you.'

'You want me to say I forgive you?'

Rachel shook her head. 'No. I suspect that would be asking too much. I just wanted to —'

'Were you and Oscar happy together?' Harriet interrupted.

If Rachel was surprised by the interruption and the question, she didn't show it. 'Yes. Although the last five years were, let's say, a challenge.'

'I've been happy too with Frank,' Harriet said. 'I suspect probably happier than if Oscar and I had stayed married. Ellie tells me you're returning to France soon.'

'That was the plan. I may be staying now. Depends on how things work out,' Rachel said.

'With Johnnie?'

Rachel nodded. 'Yes, with Johnnie.'

'He's a good man,' Harriet said. 'He deserves a second chance after losing Annie. You'll need to watch yourself with Sabine though. She'll not stand by and see you hurt him.'

'I'll do my best not to hurt him,' Rachel said.

'What did you mean just now, describing the last five years with Oscar as a challenge?' Harriet asked. 'Did the drink finally get him?'

Rachel shook her head, 'No. For the last five years of his life Oscar suffered from an incurable brain disease. He had progressive supranuclear palsy.'

Listening to Rachel, Harriet felt herself go cold with grief for Oscar, a man she had once loved.

'Sixteen months ago he insisted on going to Dignitas in Switzerland. He desperately wanted to die with dignity before he became bedbound, fed through a tube and unable to communicate with anyone. Having to use a wheelchair more and more was bad enough for him.'

Harriet bit her lip. Part of Oscar's attraction for her all those years ago had been the way he'd grabbed at life with all his might, bouncing back immediately on the rare occasions life didn't play fair with him. She could imagine the frustration and unhappiness he would have felt at his inability to bounce back from life's final blow.

'That must have been hard on you, as well as on Oscar,' Harriet said.

'It was, but he was suffering so much by then it seemed the right, the only, thing to do.' Rachel searched in the pocket of her jacket for a tissue and wiped her eyes.

'Have you told Ellie this?' Harriet asked gently.

'Not yet. I couldn't find the words when she came to see me. I will next time. Right, I'd better go.'

Harriet surprised herself by moving closer to Rachel and giving her a quick hug. 'You know I was on my way out when you arrived? I was on my way to talk to you,' Harriet said. 'To see if we could at the very least be civil to each other. Looks like we can.' She took a deep breath.

'It's Ellie's thirtieth birthday party at the end of the week. I know she would like you to come. Will you?'

'You mean it? I'd love to. Thank you, Harriet. I'll see you then.'

Chapter Forty-Seven

Ellie

The day before her birthday, Ellie was at home alone, Harriet having dragged Frank off to Torquay to do some last-minute shopping for the party.

Ellie had printed out Amy's manuscript again, this time complete with her own finishing chapters added and was out on the terrace giving it a read-through. She had an hour and a bit before BB came for coffee and wanted to check the chapters she'd added flowed seamlessly from Amy's, before showering and changing into more respectable clothes.

The clanging of the house bell jolted her out of the story. BB already? Had she been so engrossed in the story that the time had just disappeared? She glanced at her watch. No, BB wasn't due for another half an hour. If it was someone trying to sell something, she'd give them short shrift, that was for sure.

'Miss Lewis?'

She eyed the man standing in front of her suspiciously as she nodded, aware that he was taking in every detail of her frayed cut-off jeans and the ancient camisole vest she'd flung on that morning. Dressed to receive visitors she was not. 'You are?'

'Nick Walters. We spoke on the phone about Cassandra James.'

'Oh!' This man's voice over the phone hadn't prepared her for how deliciously sexy he was in the flesh. 'Oh!'

'Lost for words? And you a writer. Tut-tut.'

A sense of humour to go with those sexy looks.

'You could have phoned to say you were coming,' she said.

'Yeah, I'm sorry about that,' Nick said. 'Last-minute change of plan.'

Ellie opened the door wider. 'You'd better come in.'

She led the way out to the terrace. 'You can wait out here while I go and change into something ... something else.'

'Don't change on my account. Looks fine from where I am,' Nick said, laughing.

'Five minutes. Sit. Admire the view.'

Ellie raced upstairs. She'd intended to wear one of her old office outfits when she met Nick Walters for the first time. Business-like and professional. Instead he'd found her looking more like a beach bum. No time for a shower but at least she could put on something less provocative.

She grabbed a pair of jeans and a long-sleeved pink shirt out of the wardrobe. Some lipgloss, a quick comb of her hair and she was ready to fight for her rights to the last Cassandra James book.

Nick Walters wasn't admiring the view when she went back out to the terrace. He was busy reading the manuscript she'd left lying on the table. He looked up as she appeared.

'You wrote the last two chapters?'

'Yes.' No way was she going to ask if he approved of them.

'They're good.'

'Thanks.'

Nick put the typewritten sheets back on the table. 'Do you have an agent?'

'You told me not to talk to agents or publishers, so I haven't. Yet.'

'Good. In that case, meet your new agent. We'll discuss the details over dinner tomorrow.'

'Sorry, can't do that,' Ellie said, keeping a straight face with difficulty while relishing a chance to tease him. 'I'm busy tomorrow evening.'

Before Nick could say anything, the noise of the bell vibrated throughout the house.

'That'll be my friend,' Ellie said. 'I'll just let him in.'

Walking back out to the terrace with BB, she said, 'Nick Walters meet BB, a recently discovered American cousin many times removed.'

To BB she said, 'Nick has just offered to be my literary agent. Isn't that great?'

'Congratulations.'

'She's turned down my dinner invite for tomorrow though, so I might take the offer back,' Nick said. 'Says she's busy.'

'It's true,' Ellie protested. 'Tell him, BB.'

'She sure is busy tomorrow night,' BB said. 'If you ask her nicely, she'll maybe let you tag along.'

Nick looked at Ellie.

'If you'd like to come to a birthday party here tomorrow night you'd be welcome. I'm sure we'd find a moment or two to discuss things.'

'Thanks. I'll look forward to it,' Nick said, picking up the manuscript from the table. 'I'll take this and read it properly. Bring it back tomorrow with my suggestions.'

'I wanted to edit it some more before I showed it to you,' Ellie protested. 'It wouldn't need any suggestions from you then.'

'Rule No.1: Authors listen to what their agent has to say, inwardly digest it, and then argue their case. After which the agent may change their mind but, mainly, the author bows to their superior knowledge. Okay?'

'Are you going to be a bossy agent?'

'Of course. Now, what time tomorrow night?'

'About 7.30,' Ellie said.

'I'll see you then. Nice to meet you, BB. I'll find my own way out. Ciao.'

'Ciao,' Ellie muttered.

'Think you've got yourself one sassy agent there, Ellie,' BB said, laughing at the expression on Ellie's face.

Chapter Forty-Eight

Harriet et al.

Harriet sighed with satisfaction looking out over the garden. Although sadly the roses had finished and the summer flamboyance of colourful plants had died back somewhat, it was still looking good. Frank had placed the half-dozen tall torch candles they'd bought yesterday around and she'd hung candles in jars from various branches. Already lit, they were starting to cast a shadowy, magical ambience over the garden. Later, the full moon would add its own special silver light to the atmosphere.

The terrace too had candles as well as the solar-powered lights they'd placed in the wall over summer. Fixed to the brick side wall at the end of the terrace was a banner. 'Happy 30th Birthday Ellie'. The birthday cake with its thirty candles was in the old-fashioned larder. Extra bottles of champagne were in the fridge ready for a toast.

Frank was already busy, hovering over the BBQ like a master chef, feeding people. The trestle table alongside was full of pork soaked in a spicy marinade, lamb kebabs, sausages and chicken legs still waiting to be cooked. Jacket potatoes cooked in the Aga were wrapped in foil keeping warm at the back of the BBQ.

'Looking good. Just like the old days,' Sabine said, appearing at Harriet's side. 'I see Johnnie and Carla are here with Rachel.'

'You made your peace with her yet?'

Sabine nodded. 'Funny how time has the effect of mellowing things, isn't it?'

'You happy with Rachel stepping into your shoes to help with Carla while you're away?'

'Johnnie's happy so I can accept that.'

'Where's Owen?' Harriet asked, looking around.

'Getting some food and talking to BB. Apparently we sail on the 18th and there are lots of things to organise.'

'I'll miss you,' Harriet said. 'When do you reckon you'll be back?'

'If Owen gets his way, next March. Just in time for the summer.'

'You'll be able to see a lot of the world in that time.'

'I'm going to miss all this,' Sabine said, waving her hand in the direction of the garden and river. 'I've never been away for longer than a fortnight.'

'Owen will make sure you don't get too homesick,' Harriet said. 'There's always Skype too.'

Sabine nodded.

'Frank wants to sell up Cirencester, retire and move here permanently,' Harriet said. 'So I'll definitely be here when you get back.'

'Ellie too?'

'Yes. Unless a certain Nick Walters entices her away to live in London.' Harriet looked over at the corner of the garden where Ellie was laughing at something Nick had said. 'I have a feeling that she may have finally met "the one" for her.'

'I've left her a present in the kitchen. Shame I didn't know about him.'

Harriet glanced at her curiously.

'You'll see. Right. I'm going to go and get some of that delicious-looking food Frank is cooking.'

An hour later, after Ellie had cut her birthday cake accompanied by a loud champagne-fuelled rendition of 'Happy Birthday', Harriet made her way to the corner of the garden near the house, where Frank had recently placed a bench. By day it had one of the best views up river. By night, the lights along the river banks and on the river itself were mesmerising.

Sabine, carrying two glasses and a champagne bottle, joined her a few moments later.

'Is it an "I want to be alone" moment? Or can I join you?'

Harriet patted the seat next to her. 'Sit. I was just gathering myself together for the last hour or so,' Harriet said. 'Don't seem to have the stamina to party the night away these days.'

'Me neither.' Sabine poured two glasses of champagne. 'This will help though.'

As they sipped their drinks, Ellie appeared. 'Mum, you have to come and see what Sabine has given me. It's wonderful.' She turned to Sabine.

'Thank you so much. It's a picture I'll always treasure.'

Harriet stood up. 'Sabine has painted you a picture? Lucky girl. Where is it?'

'In the kitchen. And it's infinitely more than a picture,' Ellie said.

Looking at the painting two minutes later, Harriet had to agree. It was an artistic masterpiece of their life in Dartmouth.

Sabine had painted a modern genre picture of the Royal Avenue Gardens in all its summer glory. A band playing in the bandstand, couples dancing, children playing and people standing around watching. Recognisable people.

'Look, this is me standing under the archway watching everybody. There's you, Mum, dancing with Dad. There's Johnnie and Carla in her pushchair. BB is with them. I think that's Aunt Amy sitting on the bench eating an ice cream. See that couple there,' Ellie pointed to a couple Sabine had placed to the back and slightly to the left in the painting. 'That's Rachel and Oscar. Oh this is so brilliant.'

'There are other local people in there too that you'll get to know now you're living here,' Sabine said. 'I'm sorry I didn't know about Nick in time to paint him in.'

'That is a shame,' Ellie agreed. 'Otherwise it represents all the people that are important in my life. I must go show Dad and everyone.' Holding the picture carefully, she was gone.

'You're so talented,' Harriet said. 'That painting is something else. Somehow you've captured the essence of all our pasts and combined it with promise for the future.'

'Thank you,' Sabine said. 'Have to say I'm rather proud of it.' She hesitated before continuing. 'When we get back from our travels, Owen thinks I should concentrate on my painting. Not work the kiosk for him.'

'You should so do that, Beeny,' Sabine said. 'You have such talent.'

'Think I've left it a bit late in life to take the art world by storm though,' Sabine said.

'Nonsense.'

'That's what Owen says. Oh and by the way, you were right. He threw out my idea of being "friends with benefits" straight away when I mentioned it. Said he wanted marriage or nothing. Then he proposed again.'

'And?'

Sabine smiled. 'This time I said yes.'

EPILOGUE

It had been a good summer in the end. The weather had been kind with more sun than rain. Tourists had come in their droves. Locals had endured the daytime crowds and traffic before coming out in the evenings to saunter along the quay, enjoying their town when it was quieter.

Whilst fortunes hadn't been made, the holidaymakers had spent enough of their hard-earned cash in the town and the townspeople could relax knowing there was enough money in the bank to tide them over winter.

Best of all, there was good news about the kiosk. The week after half term, when workmen arrived to dismantle the summer-weary kiosk, people stood around smiling and watching the symbol of summer being un-ceremoniously loaded onto a lorry, safe in the knowledge that next summer it would be back.

In the end there had been no need for a public meeting or a petition. The council had simply announced a change of heart. The little kiosk by the sea was safe.

If you loved *The Little Kiosk by the Sea* then turn the page for an exclusive extract from *Rosie's Little Café on the Riviera*, another sparklingly brilliant romance from Jenifer Bohnet!

Chapter One

'*Bonne chance,*' the notaire said, counting the large wad of euros Rosie had given him before pushing a bunch of keys across the desk towards her. 'The Café Fleur is now yours.'

Five minutes later and, juggling the keys happily, Rosie walked along the ancient ramparts edging the Mediterranean towards the beach and the Café Fleur. Day one of the rest of her life was here at last and it felt oh so good. It had seemed to take forever, but one of her lifelong dreams was about to become a reality.

Owning and running her own successful café had been her number-one dream for several years now. Her other dream of being married and having a family by the time she was thirty had been foiled by her own seeming inability to build a long-lasting relationship with any man.

It was after a wine-fuelled thirtieth-birthday hangover that she'd decided enough was enough. Life was passing her by. Okay, she'd failed to meet and marry Mr Right, but owning her own café was still within her grasp. So, Dream Target No. 1 became saving enough money to open her own beach café in the South of France. Now, a couple of months before her thirty-fifth birthday, she was about to realise her dream.

Glancing across the bay to where several boats were making their way to the marina entrance, her smile faded. She recognised the hull of the boat leading the way, flying the English ensign. *A Sure Thing*, the yacht she'd been chef on for the past few years, while she squirrelled away enough money to gain her independence, was returning to port.

Briefly she wondered if Antoine, the skipper, had forgiven her yet for deserting him. He'd been less than happy when she'd told him her plans.

'*Sacre bleu*, Rosie, Charlie's going to be furious when he finds out you've left. He'll probably make William fire me for letting you go. Rosie, please, for me – one more summer?'

'No. Definitely not.' Rosie shrugged. 'He already knows I've left but, Antoine, *do not*, under any circumstances, tell Charlie the whereabouts of my restaurant. Understood?'

Antoine had given her a resigned nod and wished her well, knowing when he was beaten.

Rosie sighed. She could only cross her fingers and pray that the message had got through to Charlie that she wasn't interested in a relationship, however much he wanted to rekindle their long-ago college affair. She had enough to do getting the Café Fleur ready to open without having to deal with him as well.

Hopefully the yacht was coming into port to take on fuel and stock up with food supplies and wouldn't be staying long. Maybe they had plans to motor across to Corsica, one of Charlie's favourite places. Corsica would be good. Go to Corsica, Rosie silently willed.

The longer she could keep the location of her new business from Charlie, the better. The scene he was sure to make when he realised what she was doing was not one she looked forward to. Not that she cared these days what he thought, but no way did she want him turning up at her opening party next week. He definitely wasn't on the guest list.

Tansy, ex-stewardess on *A Sure Thing*, her best friend and, as of today, her sous-chef, waitress and chief washer-upper, was waiting for her in the car park at the back of the restaurant. 'Signed your life away?'

'Yep – and I've got the keys to prove it,' Rosie said, stretching to raise the security grill before putting the first key in a lock near the top of the door and turning it. Another large, old-fashioned key went into a lock in the middle of the door and finally she bent down to insert a small, gold-coloured key into the lock six inches from the bottom, before turning the handle and opening the door.

'I guess the last guy had a security obsession,' she said. 'At least, I hope that's all it was.'

Inside, dusty tables and chairs were arranged in neat rows, a pile of parasols leaned haphazardly against the far wall and faded curtains hung limply at the sides of the shuttered windows. In the kitchen a huge, old, white-doored fridge, which looked ancient enough to have graced Elizabeth David's kitchen fifty years ago, held centre stage. Its presence dwarfing all the other, equally old, utensils. Rosie prayed it would all be in working order once she and Tansy had cleaned things.

No way could she afford to buy a lot of new equipment. Paying the notaire had seriously depleted her bank account. She needed to be open and putting money into her new business account as quickly as possible. Otherwise she would be in trouble financially before the season even got going.

'Right, let's get the shutters open and make a start,' Rosie said.

'What's behind that door?' Tansy asked, pointing to a door at the side of the bar.

'Stairs to a store room,' Rosie said. 'I didn't take much notice, to be honest, I was more interested in down here. Come on, let's get scrubbing.' She handed Tansy a pair of pink rubber gloves before pulling on a pair herself.

While Tansy got to grips with the kitchen, Rosie went through to make a start on the restaurant. Sliding the bolts back on the front door, she stepped out onto the terrace to fold back the shutters with their peeling Provençal blue paint and stood for a few moments, visualising it busy with customers. *Her* customers. Eating outside on the terrace was an essential part of her plan for the café. People loved eating al fresco.

Two large eucalyptus trees gave some perfumed shade where the terrace ran down to the beach. The French phrase *pieds en mer* – feet in the sea – described it perfectly, Rosie thought, looking around. Oleander bushes already budding up. Yachts sailing in the distance. A woman and a young girl beach combing. Shimmering sea.

A vine with a thick, tree-like trunk covered the loggia running along the length of the restaurant. Rosie sighed. It really was an amazing location come true for her dream. It had to be a success for so many reasons. Not least because it was her final chance to make something of herself. And of course there was the little matter of being bankrupt if she didn't make it work. She took a deep breath. Failure was simply not an option.

The Beach Hotel next door was undergoing a seasonal spring clean too, judging by the number of men carrying ladders, paint, new equipment, etc. who were swarming all over it. Rosie watched enviously as three men struggled to manoeuvre a large La Cornue range through a narrow door on the side of the building. That was a stove to die for. Pity her budget didn't allow for gadgets like that.

What couldn't she do to this place if she had a 'no limits' budget? New tables and chairs – some of those comfy, Paris bistro-type ones indoors, teak ones outside. New modern equipment in the kitchen. An up-to-date range. Different crockery and cutlery, pretty tablecloths, a florist to come in every day with fresh flower arrangements, rather than the silk ones she was planning to use. Original paintings on the wall – ah, but she was going to have those. Tansy knew someone who wanted to hang some paintings of local scenes, and a few exotic ones, with a view to selling them, so hopefully every few weeks the paintings would change.

A man sitting on the rocks down by the shoreline smiled and raised a hand in greeting. Rosie hoped he didn't make a habit of sitting in front of her café – with his bare feet, tousled, sun-bleached hair, cut-off jean shorts, and a pink T-shirt bearing the faded word MUSTIQUE, he didn't exactly fit the image she had of the customers she wanted in her café. Like he'd ever been there. Neither did she want his presence to attract any undesirable friends he might have.

Rosie politely raised her hand in acknowledgement but didn't make eye contact, hoping he'd take the hint she didn't want to talk. He didn't.

'Hi, I'm Sebastian. Seb to most people,' he said, walking towards her and extending his hand, the leather friendship bracelets around his wrist tangling as they dropped forward. Reluctantly Rosie shook his hand. She didn't want to be rude but she didn't intend to encourage him to hang around.

'I'm Rosie.'

'Restaurant reopening soon? The old place could do with a makeover.'

'A week today,' she said.

'Have you got all the staff you need? I might be able to help if you haven't.'

His English was impeccable but tinged with a faint accent some people might have described as sexy. Did he want a job? Or was he just asking, making conversation? He probably didn't even have any suitable work clothes and, while the dress code during the day in her restaurant might be casual, she certainly wasn't going to allow the staff to dress tattily. In the evenings, dress would definitely be smart casual.

'All organised, thank you,' Rosie answered quickly. He didn't need to know Tansy was the only staff she could currently afford. Looking at Seb's tanned, olive skin and the general air of casualness that hung about him, she guessed he'd be more of a drifter than a steady nine-to-five-type guy.

'Look, I'm sorry, but I really do have to get on,' she said. 'So much to do.' This time he took the hint.

'Yeah, right. See you around,' Seb said with a smile and wandered off along the beach.

'Good luck,' she called out, feeling unexpectedly guilty about not being more friendly towards a guy who was clearly down on his luck. If he came back, she would definitely offer him a couple of small jobs – cleaning the windows or washing the terrace down, something like that.

Seb didn't turn round at her words, merely waved his hand in the air in acknowledgement.

Back in the restaurant, Rosie set to work. She pushed the old upright piano in the corner by the French windows into the centre of the room, making a mental note to check the piano tuner was still coming Saturday morning. Musical lunches and suppers were all part of her plan to create a different ambience in the restaurant. And live music for the party was a definite necessity.

Three hours later, when Tansy made them both a coffee from the newly cleaned espresso machine that had sprung miraculously, if noisily, into life when she switched it on, they were both fit to drop.

'Rob said he'd give us a hand painting tomorrow if you'd like him to,' Tansy said, smothering a yawn.

'Great,' Rosie said. 'I was going to make a start this evening but...' She glanced at her watch. 'I think I'll just make a list of things I've got to get at the cash-and-carry on Thursday. Rob still okay about us borrowing his van?'

'I've got to drop him off at the marina first, then we've got the van until three o'clock. Right, I'm off. See you in the morning.'

Closing the door behind Tansy, Rosie stood by the kitchen window for a few moments watching the continuing activities at the hotel. A large poster had been placed in one of the upstairs windows overlooking their car park: GRANDE RÉOUVERTURE BIENTÔT.

Just how grand would their opening be? And how soon was soon? Would she be open before they were? Was she about to find herself in competition with a top-notch chef right on her doorstep? Would their food be better than hers? Rosie shook herself. She would not think negative thoughts.

The advertisement she'd arranged on the local English radio station would hopefully bring a few ex-pats her way and kick-start a word-of-mouth buzz about the Café Fleur before the summer tourists started to arrive.

She'd worry about the competition next door when she knew more about it.

ACKNOWLEDGEMENTS

Thanks to Charlotte Mursell and the team at HQ – couldn't have done it without you. A big thank-you must also go to the online forum of HQ authors for their friendship and support. No names, no pack drill, but you know who you are! Thank you.

HQ
One Place. Many Stories

The home of bold, innovative
and empowering publishing.

Follow us online

 @HQStories

 @HQStories

 HQStories

 HQ Stories

 HQMusic